Reptile

Jeremy Eads

Unveiling Nightmares Ltd

Copyright © 2024 by Jeremy Eads

All rights reserved.

No portion of this book may be reproduced in any form without written permission from the publisher or author,

except as permitted by U.S. copyright law.

Cover Design – Carmilla Mayes

Tate, Ryan, Merryn, and Siobhan – Follow your dreams unapologetically.

And to my mother – We're still rolling along.

Contents

1. Book I	1
9. Book II	166
15. Book III	264
About the Author	347
Acknowledgements	348
The Lodge	349

Book I
Reptile

With the coming dark the change would be upon him soon. It was getting easier. He stood naked by the window waiting for the sun to set, his senses becoming hypersensitive. His mother snored softly in front of the television downstairs, two floors beneath him. Dogbone, his white German shepherd, also slept unaware. Outside, a skunk investigated the pen where the trash cans were kept. That one he both heard *and* smelled.

The sun sank a little lower – barely a fiery sliver behind the evergreens now, burning its hydrogen into the void, sinking lower and a little lower still. The moon, rising low and dirty in a sky the color of a deep bruise would be full tonight. He stretched. The change was closer with the coming dark.

He opened the door leading to a rooftop deck. Better to do it now. The sun finally dipped below the mountains. Raising his arms to the sunless sky, he embraced the change. The tingling began in his neck and ran down his back, like blue flame down his spine. His body prickled and burned as nerves shifted and realigned. His neck extended; his facial bones broke and reformed. He fell to the floor and crawled toward the outside air.

His fingers and toes extend, gaining an extra knuckle each. Shining silver claws burst from the tips with little dribbles of crimson. His spine elongates freeing his tail. With a groan that was more a reptilian hiss, black leathery wings burst from his back. New muscles grew, stretching to accompany the new appendages.

Why had he thought this was getting easier?

Crawling on all fours, mindful not to scratch up the floor, he makes his way out to the deck. Realizing something is wrong Bone is now scratching outside the door, whining, wanting to help. Mother snores on, unaware. Relishing the newfound power in his limbs and the cool night air on his scales, he filled his lungs with it and extended his wings. Then he leapt off the deck.

It was time to hunt.

Mark Branton sat tracing the path of a dust mote with the tip of his pencil. The last hour of the last day of the school year was the worst. This year it was particularly bad because he was in his final hour of middle school. Next year he'd be a freshman at Summit Valley High. A fresh fish. Like a fish the dust mote danced and twisted on invisible air currents, highlighted in the afternoon sun.

"Mark."

If he was a little slower, he could touch the mote with the tip of his pencil. He could catch the fish. Sure he could. It twisted teasingly, a tiny glowing curl. He was so close...

"Mark!"

Almost. The movement of his pencil must be creating a disturbance because the mote always flittered away right before he could touch it.

"Mark!"

Startled out of his next attempt, Mark jumped in his desk, cheeks going hot. The entire class was staring at him.

Someone murmured, "What a tool."

"Yes, Mrs. Connor." Guilt and embarrassment dripped from his mumbling mouth. Why couldn't she leave him alone?

"I know there are only a few minutes left, but do you think you could at least do me the courtesy of *pretending* to listen?" Mrs. Connor, his homeroom teacher, young and pretty-ish in a severe way. Her husband taught science down the hall. Rumor was they would both be moving to teach at the high school next year. Not that it mattered to Mark.

"Yes Mrs. Connor."

All Mark wanted to do was make it through the last fifteen minutes and then home. Mrs. Connor resumed her end of year speech about life beyond cell phones and how she hoped they would do some reading over the break. She kept her eye on him though. Probably thinking what a sad strange boy he was. Mark would do plenty of reading, his favorite escape. But today, reading wasn't on his mind.

He was going camping when he got home. His mother had already given permission for him to go. Summer, for Mark, began with a couple days of him in the woods- if you considered Coopers Cave the woods- surviving on his own. He was a bit worried leaving Mom alone, but she told him she survived before he was born and she'd be fine for the next couple of days. Mark couldn't wait.

He was beginning to think the clock was broken. Or maybe running backward. How long did it take for fifteen minutes to pass, anyway? Mrs. Connor continued talking about their upcoming high school careers and what a wonderful time it was going to be in their lives. She would talk right up to the bell and beyond if the students let her. Mark thought nothing pleased Mrs. Connor more than the sound of her own voice.

Their final report cards lined up in order by row on the table next to the door. When the bell rang, Mrs. Connor dismissed the class row by row. Each student would grab their report card and made their way out to the summer sunshine and freedom. Mark sat in the middle of the last row. He would be one of the last one's out the door.

The students seemed to be moving even slower than the clock. How hard was it to pick up a piece of paper? On top of that it seemed like every student suddenly had something profound to say to Mrs. Connor before departing.

Mark's row was called. He shot up out of his seat, grabbed his report card off the table, mumbled a swift "K, bye" when Mrs. Connor wished him a good summer, and made his way into a hallway already chock-full of screaming celebratory middle schoolers drunk on summer's possibility.

Hustling down the steps in time with the flood of kids around him, Mark waited until on the street opened his report card. Once the school was behind him Mark checked his grades. His mother didn't make a big deal of report cards because he was a good student, if a tad lazy, and his grades were usually acceptable. She knew there wouldn't be any hidden surprises in the envelope. Three As, science, government, and English, two Bs in math and coding, and a C in physical education might not get him into Harvard, but they weren't going to get him in trouble either.

"See ya in high school pusssssaaaaaayyyyy!"

A bottle, thrown from a speeding Mustang, hit Mark squarely in the back of the head. Being hit unexpectedly with an object thrown from a car moving at least forty miles an hour tends to take a guy off his feet. Mark hit the street without enough time to break his fall. Asphalt had scraped his nose and forehead. Mark felt a lump already swelling on the back of his head. Tires screeched and a flash of red disappeared around the corner. At least it was heading down 5th street toward downtown away from him.

The bottle had shattered on impact with his skull. Mark spent the rest of his walk picking shards of glass out of his hair and scalp, skull bleeding both front and back. Mark removed his gym uniform from his bag which were still sweaty from his last middle school gym class, then used his shirt to dab at his nose and forehead and the shorts to slow the blood from the bottle wound. It was humiliating enough that he'd been blindsided, and he drew the line at wiping his face with his sweaty shorts.

His mother might go completely sideways when she saw the condition of his clothes. The shirt he was wearing was probably ruined, tacky with drying blood it stuck to his chest and his back. This was one of his good shirts, and they didn't have the money to go out and buy new clothes whenever they wanted. True, it wasn't his fault, but that wouldn't matter when his mother burst into tears at the thought of the expense of new clothing. They didn't have much and Mark tried to take care of the things he had but sometimes, life happened. It came out of nowhere, busted you in the head, ruining your good clothes. Mom would look at his shirt, now a bloody rag, and cry.

She'd try to hide it, which made it worse, because he always knew. Through no fault of his own, he would make his mother cry. He just couldn't think of a good way to hide his ruined clothes. She kept track of his things. Often, she knew where his stuff was when he didn't. Trashing the shirt didn't seem viable. She would know if he got rid of it. She would want to know what happened.

He couldn't lie to her - not to Mom. She worked way too hard, sacrificed too much. Dad tried to make things better for them by joining the Army. A roadside bomb in Iraq ended that dream. When he died, every good thing they had died with him.

Mom had been working at the Wells Fargo bank, but they fired her when she needed time off for the funeral. Unable to find another job that paid as well, Mom took a job as a waitress at Chuck's on First downtown. Even though it was full time, she didn't make much. Without Army money there never seemed to be enough to pay all the bills. Every month his mother pulled a little further away from him. She cried more. She smiled less. And didn't laugh at all.

He tried to help by shoveling driveways in the winter and cutting lawns in the summer. Winter had been relatively mild this year and there wasn't any extra. Spring yielding to summer meant Mark had a plan to expand the number of houses he worked. Having a riding mower would have been ideal. Dad talked about getting one when he came back from deployment. Dad talked about a lot of things which never happened.

Pushing his mower around Caseknife, into downtown, and the surrounding neighborhoods was hot, hard, sweaty work. Riding a mower would have been so much better. Mark had no choice but to suck it up and push that pig up and down the mountain.

He would do it to help his mother. Maybe the extra money he brought in would bring her back to him. He'd give anything to hear her laugh again.

Mark would be in high school next year - practically a man - and it was time for him to start taking care of his family. Dad always said a man takes care of his own. Well, they were the only family they had, and he would take care of her. She'd see. Maybe he'd replace his shirt himself so she wouldn't have to worry about it.

Mark stood at the base of his driveway, looking up the long gravel stretch to where his house perched overlooking Caseknife Road. Lost in thought he'd walked the two and a half miles from school without noticing

His grandparents built his house in the twenties and raised his dad there. They moved in when his grandfather died, and for a time they were a happy foursome – Mark, Mom, Dad, and Grandma. Grandma passed two years after Pawpaw. Dad joined the Army not too long after. He said salvation for their family lay in the military. Medical, dental, and vision insurance along with steady pay would pull them up from poverty.

Mark started his fourth-grade year with both parents. At the start of his fifth-grade year he no longer had a father. Some guy in a country Mark hadn't heard of ruined his and his mother's life with a bomb. The two of them rattled around in the house his Pawpaw built, two shell-shocked peas at the bottom of the can.

Most days Mark enjoyed the sound of gravel crunching under his shoe as he made his way up the driveway. Today all he wanted was to get in and get out. He'd been hoping mom was already gone. Their old Toyota truck rested in the yard. It had belonged to his dad, probably why Mom wouldn't get rid of it even with paint peeling off rusted metal. Faded gray cloth on the ceiling hung in delicate bits and tatters. The stained upholstery had worn thin. It died when she put it in reverse and above sixty miles an hour caused it to shimmy and shake hard enough to vibrate out fillings. Granted, it seldom had reason to move so fast.

The truck had over two hundred thousand miles. It was over twenty years old - a classic- but she wouldn't part with it. Once the muffler fell off while they were on a special birthday dinner for Mark in Roanoke. Mark, along with a concerned stranger, crawled underneath it to hang the muffler back with coat hanger wire. Mom bought a new muffler bracket the following week and the two of them figured out how to put it back on, together.

Now the truck sat in the yard, an early warning system, letting Mark know Mom was indeed home. Maybe if he rushed to the washer, he could get it in with the laundry before she saw it. If she wasn't in the kitchen Mark could make it. Feeling hopeful again he reached for the door handle. The door pulled away from him and Mark almost fell again.

Sabrina Branton was about to leave for the second half of her shift. If he'd walked a little slower, he would have missed her entirely.

But no.

"Hey there high school- Oh my God! Mark!" She rushed forward, taking his face in her hands, her fingers accidently brushing the cut on the back of his head tearing it open and making him bleed again. Wincing at the fresh blossom of pain, Mark jerked away from her touch. "Baby! My *baby*! What happened to your head?"

"It's okay, Mom. I'm okay."

"You're not ok! Look at you! You're bleeding everywhere! Your whole head is bleeding!"

"I fell walking home. That's all."

"What about the back of your head?" She pinched his jaw to turn his head surveying the damage. "This might need stitches!"

Mark had to put the brakes on before it spiraled out of control. He wasn't going to let a bully ruin his first days of summer and probably the only freedom he would have for three months.

"I don't need stitches Mom. I fell. That's all. No way am I going to spend any of my camping time at the doctor."

"You'll go to the doctor if I say you need it, young sir. Now, go get changed and cleaned up and we'll see how you look after that."

Mark gratefully took his cue to exit, went to the bathroom, and stripped off the dirty clothes. He thought about running a bath but decided on a shower, to save time, instead. He gingerly washed the back of his head, noting with mild alarm how much blood was washing down the drain. If his head wouldn't quit bleeding he'd be in the doc's office for sure. After forever, the water finally ran clear.

Mark got out of the shower drying off with slow deliberate motions. He was particularly gentle around the back of his head so as not to get the wound weeping again. His forehead, like the tip of his nose had some small scrapes, nothing terrible. The lump on the back of his head, split and bloody, had been scary. Wrapping a towel around his waist he went downstairs to show his mother.

///

She wasn't completely convinced she shouldn't take him to the doctor for stitches. Concussion hovered at the forefront of her mind. Clearly, Mark's head took a walloping coming and going, his brain rattling around inside his skull. *He was so stubborn!* Sabrina relented after applying a layer of superglue over the nastiest cut on the back of his head. It had almost quit bleeding. The covering insured the cut was somewhat protected from dirt and nastiness. He claimed not to have a headache and had no problem recollecting his last day of middle school for her.

The last thing she needed was for him to get an infection.

///

Mark was thrilled to get out of the house without a detour for stitches. He'd deal with the rubbery lump of dry glue on the back of his head - he was already resisting the urge to dig at the edges - but that was a small price to pay. He ran upstairs, put on clean clothes, and checked his pack one more time. He had loaded everything the night before, but it never hurt to double and triple check when headed into the wild.

The bottom of his pack had his clothing, shirts, shorts, swimsuit, towels, two extra days' worth of socks and underwear, rain gear, and laundry bag. His shaving kit containing toothbrush, toothpaste, Aleve, deodorant, roll of toilet paper, 3 in 1 soap/shampoo/conditioner, comb, lighter, and toenail clippers sat on top of his clothing. Mark didn't shave but the kit had belonged to his father. Leaving without it was unacceptable.

Beside the shaving kit Mark packed a few packs of gel fire starter. Plenty of wood to burn littered the ground at the campsite. Mark didn't like to fight getting a fire going. He liked to build a fire first thing and have it going while he set up camp. Camp smoke helped clear out the bugs and by the time Mark was set up he'd be comfy and bug free. Plus, he could cook his dinner whenever and wouldn't have to wait - or worse, eat a cold meal because he was too tired to build a fire.

His ground tarp and a small pillow were stacked next along with a small tool kit. The toolkit contained a hand axe that could double as a hammer, extra stakes, work gloves, can opener, an entrenching tool that was both shovel and pickaxe, scissors, small flashlight, and a small mirror. Cans of beef stew, half a loaf of Wonder bread, a jar of extra crunchy peanut butter, a small frying pan, tongs, a couple of Whatchamacallits, a thermos full of lemonade, a shower bag, tent stakes, and a coil of rope rested on top of the pile.

Mark strapped the pack closed and tied on his tent, sleeping mat, and sleeping bag. Bottles of water as well as two Mio electrolyte water enhancing flavor drops, fruit punch and berry pomegranate, were stuffed into the net pockets on the outside of the pack along with a can of OFF! Deep Woods. With the camping gear checked and repacked Mark lifted the pack onto his shoulders testing the weight.

It weighed about a thousand pounds.

He wasn't going to put anything back, so he'd just have to suffer. Last time he had been to Coopers Cave and the Deer Hole he'd been with his dad who made carrying this stuff look easy.

Mark fastened the wimp strap around his waist and pulled the shoulder straps snug. He waddled downstairs looking like the world's tallest, palest turtle. Mark kissed his mother who looked doubtfully at him, then headed out the door before she could object. He grabbed his walking stick started across the yard toward the waiting wilderness. A short whistle, and Bone came running from the back of the house tail wagging happily at the prospect of a walk.

The weather was perfect. Warm, but not overly so, early Virginia summer bliss. Still, Mark broke a sweat even before reaching the cool shadows of the woods. Bone ventured ahead, scouting the trail, but kept looking back to make sure Mark hadn't changed direction. A barely-there trail—almost invisible unless you knew where to look—led down the hill and back up another steeper one, then disappeared around the crown.

Mark had last walked this path with his dad, who had shown him this trail and where the hidden swimming holes were—the good spots most people didn't know about. Mark knew how to track, hunt, and survive in the wild because his father had cared enough to teach him.

Dad was raised with a deep knowledge of earth craft and wood lore now mostly forgotten. He hadn't taught Mark everything, he didn't have time, but he taught Mark beyond the basics. A love of nature passed from father to son along with the desire to achieve natural harmony, equilibrium, with the land. Hidden in the Appalachian mountain scape surrounding his home were a wealth of secret vistas, waterfalls, and other natural jewels. His father shared some of his favorites before vanishing into the sand.

Coopers Cave and the Deer Hole were two such spots. The cave was nothing more than two large slabs of granite that had collapsed against each other a billion years ago. Over time, dirt had settled and grass grew on top of the rocks, leaving a comfortable "cave" protected from the elements. The angle of the stones also provided a natural chimney for campfire smoke to escape outside. The cave itself wasn't deep enough for the air to become stagnant. Coopers Cave was a perfect natural campsite.

The Deer Hole lay protected in the valley—or holler, as it's called in Summit Valley—beneath Coopers Cave. A small waterfall fed into a deep spring pool. A series of small tributaries wound their way down through the mountains, joining and separating and joining again, eventually emptying into the New River. This collection of springs and creeks was known locally as Peak Creek. The Deer Hole had a current, proof that somewhere in its depths, it was a part of Peak Creek, but the surface was deceptively still. The fishing was good. The swimming was better. But even among locals, the Deer Hole was considered a tough hike, and there were other more accessible places to get wet. Throughout the year, a dozen people might visit the Deer Hole.

Exactly why Mark loved it.

He felt like this place and Coopers Cave above belonged to him, a place he and his father had played in better times. The Deer Hole was sacred ground to Mark, and he pretended no one came back here. It was his alone now that his father was gone.

After what felt like a thousand-mile uphill march, the familiar stones of Coopers Cave came into view. Mark dropped his gear inside the cave and took a moment to shake the tension out of his shoulders. He'd managed to lug the heavy pack here without too much trouble. *Dad would be proud I made it.* Bone lay beside the gear, cooling his belly on the stone floor of the cave and panting contentedly.

Mark made a quick sweep of the area. No sign anyone had been in the cave, and a quick peek confirmed he had the Deer Hole to himself. A swim sounded fine after lugging his heavy pack up the mountain, but as much as he wanted to run down the hill and jump in the water, he knew he should set up his camp first.

Reluctantly, he turned his back to the temptation of the Deer Hole and began to gather wood for the campfire. Some early spring storms had broken branches and downed trees across the county. Mark had no trouble gathering the dried-out wood off the ground. Ten minutes saw him with enough wood to keep the fire going for his entire trip.

Mark set some branches in the stone-ringed fire pit and dug out his fire starter. He set the starter and lighter neatly beside the pit. He then set up his tent and unpacked the food. It might have been overkill to set up the tent inside the cave, but Mark felt more secure with a barrier between him and the outside world. He didn't like the feeling of being watched, and it could get creepy out here by himself in the dark.

Bone was there if anything happened, but Mark still felt better with something to break the line of sight. When the sun was high, he was okay with being alone. But when the sun set and the only light came from his little campfire, the creepiness factor went up a notch.

Mark glanced around, his eyes narrowed. The woods quieted, and even the usual background noise of birds and insects had ceased, as though the forest held its breath. *That's weird.* The hair on Mark's arms stood up, and his skin broke out in gooseflesh. He was glad he wasn't naked in the water right now. Sunlight filtered through the trees at a sharper angle like it, too, wanted away from the woods and whatever hid therein, painting the ground in splotchy shadows.

Bone stood at the mouth of the cave, alert. He didn't growl, but he was notably quiet and watchful. *He senses it too*, Mark thought. *There's something out there watching me.* Something not right. Mark stood beside Bone, looking into the woods. There was nothing to see but sun, shadow, trees, and dead leaves on the forest floor.

Nothing moved. Nothing made a sound. Still, the feeling of being watched was indisputable. But as suddenly as the feeling had come on, it left. The birds began to chirp, and the bugs resumed buzzing. Whatever threat had come had decided to leave. *Good thing too*, Mark thought. *Bone would chew a hole in you.*

Mark looked down at his dog and scratched him behind the ears. Bone had resumed panting and took the opportunity to give Mark's hand a good licking. What had just happened? Mark loved this place like nowhere else, but for a few minutes, it had seemed completely alien to him—hostile, even. Whatever the feeling was had passed, but Mark's good mood brought on from being here had vanished.

His time was almost up. The old man could feel the clock leaning on him. How long did he have? Months? Weeks? Certainly there were no more years. He watched the boy struggle under the weight of his pack. The child never quit. He fought the pack from his home, through the woods, and up the mountain without pausing to rest or ever putting the pack down. And now it seemed the boy knew he was being watched. The dog was aware of him, no doubt, but it was highly unusual for humans to sense his presence. The dog would have to be subdued. It wouldn't suit him to kill it outright. He needed to speak with the boy—a task made more difficult if the boy was raging over his dog.

Tonight, he would let the child sleep. The boy needed rest. Let him forget about being watched. A gentle push would help with that. They would speak tomorrow. The old man knew he had that much time, at least. Tomorrow would be soon enough.

Mark's eyes opened to the orange glow of warm sunlight filtering through the nylon of his tent. Stretching in his sleeping bag, he couldn't remember the last time he'd slept so well. Bone pounced on his chest, licking his face good morning. "Ugh! Get off me, Bone!"

Mark rolled over and unzipped the door enough for Bone, who streaked out the opening and bounded into the woods. Mark didn't worry; he knew Bone wouldn't go far. He'd be back as soon as he smelled breakfast cooking. Speaking of, Mark was pleasantly surprised to find he still had fire in the pit. He thought it would have burned out during the night, but there was enough of a flame left that all he needed to do was pile on more wood.

Ten minutes later, he had a nice fire going and a can of beef stew warming. Mark had remembered to bring the coffee, and the pot heated in the coals. Even though he didn't drink coffee, he thought it was a good way to honor his father. Dad always drank coffee.

Bone smelled the stew and came back from wherever he was for breakfast. Mark obliged him and scooped half the can into his dog bowl. The other half, he ate out of the can. After breakfast had been eaten and the dishes cleaned, Mark decided to head to the Deer Hole for the swim he'd put off the day before.

The morning sun warmed his skin as Mark bounded down the hill with Bone close behind. Without hesitation, Mark dove into the water, relishing the icy shock. He took a slow lap around the perimeter and back around again to pull up under a small waterfall. Bone alternated between following Mark's progress around the edge and lying on a rock, enjoying the sun. He seemed a little wary to Mark. On edge. The crawly sensation of being watched flashed through Mark's mind, there and gone before he could make the connection but leaving him feeling exposed and vulnerable.

No longer in the mood to swim, Mark made his way back up the hill to his camp at a considerably slower pace than he'd went down. Bone strolled along beside him, ever watchful. The rest of the day, Mark didn't do much of anything. He didn't stray from camp, hike, or go swimming again. He wasn't in the mood to fish. All he wanted to do was relax.

Lunch was out of a can and split with Bone. Mark ate but didn't really taste it. He took a nap with the tent door open. Morning heat broke into a mild afternoon, and afternoon gave way to evening, and still, Mark stayed close to camp. Bone didn't wander either. They were both on guard against some nameless trouble they couldn't pinpoint.

Sitting in his father's chair by the fire, scratching Bone behind the ears, Mark fell asleep.

"Yes, yes, build the fire back. Night is cold. Night is dark. Must have fire."

Mark opened his eyes, his neck stiff from sleeping in an awkward position, to see an old man sitting on a log across from him busily adding wood to the fire. Then he poked the coals with a stick, sending sparks dancing into the summer night.

"Just going to sit there and watch an old man work?"

Mark was startled out of his chair, falling to the dirt.

"You don't have to snap to, but your enthusiasm is admirable. Get up, boy. Let me have a look at you now that you're awake."

Mark dusted himself off, trying to recover his dignity, face flushed with embarrassment. He stared back as the old man scrutinized him from head to toe. For some reason, Mark felt like he didn't measure up. But measure up to what? He even puffed out his chest, not that he had much of one.

The old man had the kind of weather-beaten face Mark associated with cowboys in the old Western movies his dad used to watch. Combined with the white hair and neatly trimmed beard, it was hard to determine the man's age, but Mark knew the guy was old. He wore a white button-up shirt, open at the collar, underneath a worn and dirty black vest. The vest was unadorned, with the exception of four aces over the right breast. He looked like a gambler down on his luck, a guy who'd lost it all but still believed in one big payout to break even.

"A gambler, huh? I like that. You're not far off."

Mark's jaw fell open. He hadn't said a word...

"How can you be it? It's always like this, I suppose. Each generation disapproves of the ones that follow."

What was this guy talking about? Mark wondered if he was crazy, and if he was, was it the dangerous kind? Should he have been running?

"Calm down, boy. If I wanted to hurt you, I'd have done it while you were sleeping. And start talking. You're getting on my nerves."

"S-Sorry?" Mark was confused.

The old man grunted. "Don't be sorry. Do better."

"That's exactly what—"

"Your dad used to say. I know. Boy, you radiate daddy issues."

Mark closed his mouth and stared at the stranger. Where was Bone? Mark looked around. His dog was asleep on his sleeping bag in the tent, so this guy couldn't be that bad. If there was trouble, Bone would be ready to protect him, and Bone was knocked out.

"I got something here you should take a look at. Geeky kid like you ought to love it."

The old man reached behind him, then threw a drawstring pouch at Mark's feet. There was a muffled clacking when the bag hit the stone, and despite his reservations about this stranger who seemed to be able to read his mind, Mark was curious. The crushed velvet was a pale blue, and to Mark's eye, it looked like the kind of bag he might carry dice in when playing Magic: The Gathering or Dungeons & Dragons.

"Go ahead. Open it. Pull out one figure at a time, and I bet you'll find a little of both games in there."

Mark reached down and picked up the bag. It had a weight to it that could be dice, but only if those dice were of extremely high quality. Maybe custom. Mark had his eye on a set of custom metal and stone dice on display at Comix Zone, a comic bookstore and hobby shop on Main Street. They were beautiful. Opel, who worked the counter, took them out and let him hold them once. She was about the coolest girl Mark knew—purple hair, played video games, and cranked the stereo when the owner was out.

The dice had come in a crushed velvet bag that was heavy like this one. Mark wiggled his finger into the top of the bag. The drawstrings drew in and the opening loosened. The old man had said only one at a time, and that was all right . Mark enjoyed the anticipation.

He reached in the bag and felt several oddly shaped stones. This was definitely not a bag of dice. Using his thumb and forefinger, Mark pinched out the closest figure. A small stone wolf, neck craned like it was howling at the moon, rested in his palm.

"Show it to me, boy."

Holding out his hand, Mark said, "It's a howling wolf. Pretty cool."

"I think you better look again."

Mark looked back at his palm. The howling wolf now cowered, head down and ears back, with its tail tucked tightly between its legs. The sculpture no longer resembled a proud pack hunter, but more like a cowardly sneak kicked one too many times. Mark held it up eye level, astounded. That wolf had been howling when he'd brought it out of the bag. Now Mark could almost feel the tiny sculpture shivering with fright.

"The wolf bows. Pick another." The old man held his hand out, and Mark handed him the carving. The old man motioned with his head, and as the old man set the carving down. The proud wolf was back, but its head wasn't quite as high as before.

Mark, curious before, now couldn't wait to see the next figurine. Using his pinching technique again, he reached into the blue bag. Velvet slid along the back of his hand as his hand explored deeper. His fingers grasped another cold stone. Pulling it into the light revealed a bear, strong and fierce, standing on its rear legs.

"What did you find? Show it to me!" The old man sounded as excited as Mark felt. Something was happening here, but Mark wasn't exactly sure what it meant. Bone continued to sleep as if nothing were amiss, dreaming, paws twitching.

"A bear standing on its back feet." Mark held it out.

"Better check it again, boy."

Mark looked away from the old man and into his palm. The bear was now on all fours with its head hanging down. Its mouth had closed. Mark felt the bear shying away from him. From him! Mark had never scared anyone, much less a bear. Twice now the figurines had changed without him feeling it. There had to be a trick to it, but Mark couldn't figure it out.

Coolest trick ever!

"It changed again! How are you doing it? Do you have a remote?"

"The stones choose. I have nothing to do with it. Bear yields. Choose another."

Mark didn't wait to hand the bear back. Instead, he tossed the figurine at the wolf by the old man's feet. The old man deftly caught it, snatching the figurine out of the air faster than Mark could follow, and set the bear reverently next to wolf.

"Be respectful, boy!" The old man barked.

Mark felt his cheeks grow hot with the admonishment. *The little statues must be delicate.* He sat back up and peered into the open bag. The dark opening beckoned. Mark slid his fingers into the space, feeling for the next figurine. His arm was swallowed almost to the elbow. It felt as though his hand was hanging into a great space, and this made Mark think about dangling his feet in the ocean. With the unknown beneath him, there would be no telling what manner of creature might emerge from the depths.

When his fingers found another cold stone, he pulled his arm from the bag. In his palm was a wasp. Shimmering wings stretched outward, and a black abdomen curled underneath in an attacking posture. Fearless and relentless, the wasp would attack any threat, driving it away with a barrage of painful stings.

"What now, boy? What did the bag reveal?" The old man leaned forward, eyes glowing. A gleam of perspiration glossed his face. Small beads of sweat stood out on his forehead, reflecting the firelight. A few strands of white hair had come loose, dancing off the old man's gray stubble.

Mark proudly held his hand out, but the wasp was no longer in an attack position. The statuette looked unconcerned about nearby trouble. Its wings now lay against its back, demurely covering thorax and abdomen. Head and antennae were lowered, calm and peaceful.

"Wasp yields," the old man said, almost too low to hear. "How long has it been?"

Mark shrugged off the question handing the wasp over, eager to begin another delve into the bag. The excitement hadn't faded, even with the strange words of his new camp companion. It had to be a game, and Mark wanted to see how it played out.

"Wolf, bear, and wasp have all yielded. Which will it be? Again." The man nodded toward the bag in Mark's lap. Mark didn't understand the old man's agitation. Or maybe it was fear. Was the old guy scared?

Of what? "The stones' call bid me bring them here. After you become, you'll heed the Stonesong too."

"The call of the stones?" Mark pointed at the line of figurines by the old man's chair.

"Questions later. First, listen. My name is Einar. Stop thinking of me as 'the old man.' Kind of insulting, really. I began my search after hearing the Stonesong."

"Searching for what?"

"Searching for you."

"Why?"

"The stones have chosen another. I could not know whom or for what purpose. When called, we answer. There is no option."

"You hear rocks?" Mark couldn't keep the smile off his face. The idea of listening to rocks was silly. Fairy-tale stuff. Mark had enough to deal with without talking rocks. Einar was clearly off his rocker. Over in the tent, Bone slept on, whimpering softly.

The entire scene was taking on the surreal aspects of a dream. Mark expected to wake in this chair at any moment. No old man, no bottomless bag of moving figurines, no carnival tricks, just him and Bone, camping.

Einar either hadn't heard the question or was choosing to ignore it. "Go on. Pick again." He gestured toward the bag in Mark's lap.

The black maw of the bag betrayed nothing. Mark reached again into that blackness and felt around for the next stone. His head felt stuffed with cotton, and everything felt thick and syrupy, like he was in a movie slowed to run frame by frame.

His arm had disappeared up to the elbow, and Mark was beginning to think there wasn't anything left. He was going to say as much, but Einar interrupted him: "No, boy, the bag isn't empty yet. Keep looking!"

Mark's fingertips brushed against rough stone. Stretching farther, his right arm almost completely inside the bag now, Mark managed to get his hands around the stone.

The figurine he pulled out resembled nothing he was familiar with. A snarling gargoyle with wings flared out wide bared its stony teeth at Mark. "Wow, this one is pretty cool." Mark extended the figurine to Einar. During the transition, Mark saw the figure change. The wings pulled in, and the snarl disappeared. The mouth closed as the figure crouched down on all fours, wrapping its wings protectively around itself.

"No," Einar whispered.

"What?" What was the old dude was all worked up for?

"There hasn't been a reptile for a thousand years. Maybe longer."

"A reptile?"

"Gargoyle yields. Only Lord Reptile is left." Einar placed the gargoyle beside the other cowed statuettes. "Go on, boy. Last time."

Mark knew he was going to have to work for this one. A Lord Reptile—whatever that meant. He got out of his chair, turned around, and set the limp bag on the seat. The dream feeling grew even stronger now. The fire seemed frozen in place. Sparks paused in mid-flight, hovering in the dark. The campfire smoke froze in a wispy column leading from light to nowhere—a purgatory between inferno and the heavens. In the tent, Bone slept, paws twitching.

Mark's entire right arm vanished into the bag. Then his shoulder. Mark knelt in front of his chair, reaching into an impossible void for what, he didn't know. This had to be a dream. Otherwise, he'd be terrified. Instead, he felt compelled to go along. Whatever magic slept in the bag, Mark wanted to know it, to wake it. Go along; get along. Maybe he'd fall into the bag and land as a judge in a bikini contest.

Mark felt nothing. He was going to have to put his head in the bag. *Bikini models, here I come*, Mark thought, sticking his head into the impossibly small opening. It accepted his head as easily as it had accepted the rest of him. Mark opened his eyes, dumbstruck. A galaxy—no, a group of galaxies, an entire universe spread out before him. Inside the bag existed a void beautiful beyond all description. An ordinary rock in the grass beneath his knee dug into his skin, adding to the surreal sense of being in two places at once.

The universe before the big bang must have looked something like this. Everywhere was light and motion. Mark didn't stop to think about how he was still breathing. He could sense Einar somewhere close by, and he knew he was still grounded at the campsite, thanks to the increasing discomfort in his knee. The duality made his head spin. Lost in the beauty before him, Mark forgot he was searching for something. A nagging at the back of his mind told him he should be looking for something specific but what? He'd forgotten. Did it matter? All he could do was stare in shocked disbelief. This was turning out to be the greatest dream he'd ever had—even without bikinis.

He pulled himself into the bag. Swimming amongst the stars in this micro-eternity seemed too irresistible an opportunity. He strained forward, but something had him around the waist. Maybe he wasn't going to fit through the opening after all. He twisted around. Where his waist should've been was the inner lining of the bag. Mark could feel the velvety cloth underneath his fingers. The flickering campfire was visible through the fabric.

It was Einar that held him around the waist.

"Let me go!" Mark tried to yell, but his voice disappeared into the void and was pulled away by some unknowable vacuum. Mark twisted back around again to see the stars swirling beneath him. His hand closed over something rough, and then he remembered what he was doing.

He turned, horrified now by the endless expanse beneath him. He grabbed the fabric with both hands, mindful of the stone in his right hand, and pulled. Together with Einar, he managed to get himself out of the bag, a small pop following his ungainly exit.

"Do you have it? Did you get it?" Einar whispered.

"I got this." Mark extended his hand with the stone in it.

Einar's breath drew in sharply. "I never would have thought."

The stone in his hand didn't seem remarkable. It was like the others, except shaped like a dragon. Leathery bat wings extended to their full glory, and the hind legs bunched as if rearing up, preparing to pounce. The dragon held its head at shoulder height as the long neck curled like a serpent about to strike.

Mark raised his palm toward his face for a better look. The head shot forward, propelled by a muscular neck. Tiny claws gripped Mark's cheek as the statuette bit his face. On reflex, he tried to yank the figurine away. It twisted away from his hands. Einar reached forward, running his finger down the tiny stone spine. As soon as he touched it, it became stone again—just a little figurine, not a miniature demon trying to chew its way into Mark's skull.

"Lord Reptile does not yield. It has chosen."

Mark touched his finger to the spot where the statuette had bitten him. His finger came away wet with a small spot of blood. The stone figurine in Einar's hand hadn't altered its pose as the others had. To Mark's eye, it still held the same arrogant come-at-me stance. Mark wanted to toss the evil little thing back into the void where it'd come from.

Einar, however, was staring at the bloody spot on his cheek with something akin to awe or maybe fear, and Mark wondered if the bite was worse than he thought. "Reptile has chosen," Einar whispered again. He gathered up the other statuettes and dropped them back into the bag. After looking at the reptile once more, he put it back as well.

Quickly and with much less drama than his arrival, Einar put the bag away. He put his hat back on, once again assuming the air of an old gambler. Einar walked away from the ring of firelight. A million questions buzzed through Mark's head. He was too dizzy to get up from the chair he didn't remember sitting in. His cheek stung.

And he could not seem to remember why.

His eyelids hung heavy. He must have been sleeping. Bone was asleep in the tent. The dog wasn't alarmed; Mark shouldn't be either.

Einar stood outside the ring of light thrown by the campfire, eyes blazing as he pushed the boy back into unconsciousness. Holding the dog still had been surprisingly difficult—more difficult than it should have been. *Must be getting old*. The boy had recklessly dived into the Theatre of Stones! Einar had barely caught him in time. Shaking his head at the thought of a chosen reptile floating forever lost in the void, he watched until the boy was back asleep.

Have to stop thinking of him as a boy, Einar thought. *He's the new reptile. Over a thousand years since the last, and the stone picked a small boy in this strange town.*

Einar faded into the darkness, leaving Mark to wake up and believe whatever he chose to believe.

Mark woke feeling stiff. He must have slept in the chair all night. He stood to go pee and immediately tripped over Bone. From the tingling of blood rushing back into his feet, Mark guessed Bone had been there a long time.

The rest of the time in the woods was uneventful but therapeutic for Mark. He swam, fished, and thought about his father. He loved this place—a space belonging to the two of them, even if only one was around to enjoy it. Mark spoke to his father, imagining his answers. He didn't think of Einar or the stones. He'd passed the whole episode off to a can of expired beans. *No way it could have been real*, Mark thought, absently fingering a small scab on his cheek.

///

The rest of the summer, Mark tended grass, lawn mowers, and tried not to burn. The exercise had been good for him, and the week before school began, Mark noticed he'd grown three inches, and his muscles—never what you might call impressive—had toned and hardened. And the sun had cleared up the little bit of adolescent acne he'd had.

Mark was surprised not only by how good he looked, but also how good he felt. He felt strong. Mark wasn't a physical guy. He liked to play video games. Spending a rainy day under a blanket reading by the window was a little slice of heaven Mark and his mother both enjoyed. This meant his mind was blown when, while combing his hair, he realized he'd grown actual biceps over the summer.

His mother commented on his energy and growing physique, joking that she didn't know she'd given birth to the Hulk. The extra money Mark had made mowing lawns had been enough to help cover the cost of a few new shirts and some badly needed pants and shoes.

New shoes were a must as Mark now had to walk a little farther to get to Summit Valley High School. Technically, he could have ridden the bus, but Mark preferred to walk. Dad had liked to walk. Mom did too. Mark didn't think anything of it. He could listen to music and walking in the morning helped him focus on what he needed to do each day. Walking home allowed him time to consider the day he'd had. Mark often went over the things that had gone right, wrong, and everything in between. It was healthy, a form of exercise he genuinely enjoyed, and besides, he wasn't dragging a lawn mower around. His backpack weighed almost nothing compared to the ancient grass cutter. Dad would say walking got his mind right. Mark always liked that. He walked to get his mind right too.

Mark walked down Caseknife until it turned into Commerce. A left on Commerce, up past Main Street, and all the way to Fifth Street led Mark to his next turn. Fifth would lead him past the only part of the walk he didn't like: passing the Maple Lodge. Nasty old place had always bothered Mark, and the weirdo who ran it never failed to make him uncomfortable.

Mom said to stay away, not that Mark needed any encouragement in that regard. Past the Maple Lodge, Mark crossed the street to Edgehill Drive. After that, it was a matter of following Edgehill to the high school. Then he'd do it in reverse in the afternoons. Foul weather, hard rain or snow, was the exception. In that case, Mark would ride the bus.

Walking to school made him feel close to his father. Dad had walked these same roads to these same places, and Mark felt his father with him step for step. It wasn't the same as having him, but it was nice to feel close, if only in a small way.

A red Mustang blew by as he headed up Edgehill, startling him. No bottles came flying out of it this time. Mark would have been a sitting duck; lost as he was in reverie. Lucas Gahan appeared not to have noticed him. Jerks have first-day jitters too.

Or maybe he gave Mark less thought than Mark was giving him.

Students gathered around the school. Most of them had been going to school together all their lives, and school being back in session was just another reason to socialize. Small-town kids, small-town summers, and small-town school years. There wasn't much to be nervous about when all the people you were with were the same people you'd always been with.

Lucas got out of the Mustang, Alicia Foster bouncing prettily from the passenger side. Mark liked Alicia—as a friend—and couldn't understand why she'd even considered dating Lucas in the first place. He was clearly too old for her. She was a freshman riding around with a second-year junior. She was too smart for him. Alicia outclassed Lucas in every category. Having a car and being old enough to drive must've held some attraction.

Alicia was a buddy. Back at Summit Valley Middle School, they'd eaten lunch together. They played games online. They were guildies in World of Warcraft. She played an undead mage. Mark played a Tauren warrior. Mark doubted Lucas had ever seen the Blackrock Depths or defeated hordes of undead in Stratholme. He and Alicia had many times.

Although, she hadn't been online much recently.

Mark readjusted his pack and headed inside.

Homeroom was first-day-of-school chaotic. His homeroom teacher, Mrs. Linkous, allowed the students a few minutes at the beginning of class to talk and wind down. Everyone knew she'd been doing the job nearly twenty years. She seemed to know when the kids needed a few minutes to adjust before they could be counted on to pay attention.

Mark looked around at the class. Some of the kids he knew, but most of the people in his homeroom had been at Nilbud Middle School, not Summit Valley. A guy next to him sucked a dog tag chain up his nose, then pulled it out of his mouth, flossing his sinuses.

Mrs. Linkous walked up and down the aisles, passing out schedules to the incoming freshmen. Without slowing down, she grabbed the chain, ripped it loose, and dropped it in from of him along with his schedule, then moved on without saying a word. Rubbing his nostril, the kid put his chain back in his pocket.

Back in front of the class, Mrs. Linkous explained how to read their schedules. She projected a map onto the whiteboard, displaying both floors of each pod and all the classrooms, which were labeled. Mark checked his schedule:

MWF – 0800-0930 - Algebra I – Hastings - M241

MWF – 0940-1110 – Discourse Across Disciplines – Mathews - E220

MWF – 1120-1150 – A Lunch – Admin105

MWF – 1200-1330 – Physical Education – Miller - G201

MWF – 1340-1510 – Biology I – Hagen - S220

TR – 0800-0930 – Computer Science – Introductory Typing – Ray - S140

TR – 0940-1110 – Introductory Spanish – Castlillja - E210

TR – 1120-1150 – A Lunch – Admin105

TR – 1200-1330 – Art History – Wagstaff - A205

TR – 1340-1510 – Band – Swantner - A115

His first class was Algebra I, in the math pod, second floor, room forty-one. Most of his classes were far apart, in different pods, and on the second floor. After each class, Mark would have to hustle to his locker on the first floor, then to his next class on the second floor in a short ten-minute window. Also, he had first lunch, which meant he'd be starving by the time school let out.

"Remember, students, in the spring, your schedules reverse. All your Monday, Wednesday, Friday classes will switch to Tuesday, Thursday after the new year. It's a lot to take in, but I hope you have a great year. This is your only homeroom class. In a few minutes, you'll transfer to your first period classroom, where you'll report from now on. Good luck, people."

Mrs. Linkous stood by the door, smiling as the students filed out to their first real class after summer break.

Summit Valley High School was built to incorporate both Summit Valley High and Nilbud High School into one location, saving Summit County thousands of dollars each year. A unanimous Summit Valley School Board voted to spend five million dollars on the construction of the new high school. Parents of Nilbud students weren't happy their sons and daughters were being bussed to Summit Valley to attend school with a bunch of hillbillies. Parents of Summit Valley students weren't happy their children were forced to share space with those uppity brats from Nilbud.

Neither group of parents had much recourse.

The new high school sat on five acres of hilltop near downtown Summit Valley. Five pods connected to a central administrative hub. Each pod concentrated on specific subject matter. Math and science, English and language arts, civics and history, visual and performing arts, and physical education. Seen from the air, the campus resembled a giant cog. Outside the physical education pod, a wide path led to a sunken football stadium capable of seating five thousand unruly fans. The Demon Den got wild on Friday nights from August through November when the Demons did their talking on the field.

Mark took a strange pride in the fact that his high school stadium was the only one in the state to sell beer. Budweiser trucked in kegs to the concession stands on game day as no alcohol was kept on campus. Trucks came again on Saturday morning to remove them. No other schools could boast the turnout the Demons did. Seating was sold out years in advance.

Adjacent to the Demon Den were well-maintained outdoor basketball and tennis courts. Without the same draw as the football games, parents of basketball and tennis players had to make do without beer.

Mark shuffled out behind the rest of the class, head down, staring at his schedule. Freshmen filled the halls, and faculty directed lost faces toward destinations. The hallways filled with the cacophony of slamming metal lockers, shuffling feet, rustling bookbags, and the excited chatter of the students. Cutting through the central hub of the admin building, Mark made his way to the math pod.

Since the beginning of the summer, Mark felt more alive. Aware of the world around him in a way he'd never been before. Colors seemed more vivid, leaves on the trees a deeper green. Warm summer evenings fragrant with blackberry, honeysuckle, and clover became sweeter. Even food tasted better.

Mowing lawns over the summer had produced almost overwhelming sensations. He'd felt blades of grass parting from the stalk. Vibrations from the motor traveling up both his sweaty arms as well as through the earth beneath his feet. Insects had scurried from the disturbance, creating mini earthquakes in their panic. Cut grass had mingled with the scent of blossoming honeysuckle. Mark felt like he'd been given access to a world usually unseen. Like a mysterious universe hidden in plain sight had opened to him and made itself known.

Did he have a tumor? Was it something terminal? Was some malignant cluster of cells hiding within him, waiting to snatch his life after driving him mad? Or might this be a passing thing? Mark had spent the summer working to block out his hyper awareness. If not for their need for money, he wouldn't have cut lawns at all.

That was another thing. The previous summer, he could have two lawns cut by noon if he started early enough. This summer, he'd cut five lawns before lunchtime. As July gave way to August, Mark could work through his client list on Caseknife in a day. A week's worth of work—in a day.

This included fourteen lawns every Monday—with the edging—and he would return home in the evening feeling as invigorated as if he'd just stepped out of bed. Restless at night, he'd been sleeping two hours at most. Reluctant to bring another worry to his mother, Mark kept his newfound stamina to himself. Really, it wasn't hurting anything. He felt great.

"Hey, watch me bust this bitch in the head," someone said behind him.

On reflex, Mark dropped to one knee, then pivoted one hundred and eighty degrees. His right hand flew up, snatching the bottle that had been thrown at his head mid-flight. As he sprang back to his feet, Mark's right arm swung around in a softball fast pitch, returning the bottle.

The return throw took Lucas off his feet. He sat down with a grunt, his eyes dazed, glassy. Ethan Gilmore and Lance Avery, two of Lucas's closest friends, picked Lucas up, staring wide-eyed at Mark. Neither said a word. Mark, still surprised by his own agility, stared back. Traffic in the stairwell slowed to a crawl as students looked at the goose egg rising in the middle of Lucas's head.

"Did you see that?"

"Dude's a ninja!"

"He caught it with his back turned!"

"No way! Unreal!"

The whispers spread from the stairwell and into the halls. Soon, it would be all over school. By the end of the day, the going story would be that a freshman had knocked Lucas Gahan out before first period. According to the rumor mill, Lance and Ethan were too afraid to do anything other than drag Lucas off to the nurse's office. Lucas would not be attending football practice for two weeks because of the injury to his head.

None of that was true.

"I'll see you later," Lucas said, attempting to salvage some dignity.

"Better think about it," Mark answered before turning on his heel. He made his way through silent staring faces until someone Mark didn't recognize stopped him.

"Hey, man. Did you see what happened to Lucas? I heard some kid just knocked him out!"

"Sorry, didn't see a thing. You know where Ms. Hastings's class is?"

///

Lucas sat in the nurse's office holding an ice pack to his head. Ethan and Lance had dropped him off and headed back to class. He could hear the nurse outside on the phone with his mother. They wanted to take him to the doctor in case of a possible concussion.

Humiliating.

Not only had the Branton kid knocked him silly with his own bottle, but he'd embarrassed Lucas. And nobody made Lucas Gahan look stupid. *Nobody*. Lucas did the humiliating. The burning shame he felt at being outmaneuvered fed into his constant rage, which would need to be addressed. Of course, hitting Mark in the back of the head last summer never entered his mind. So insignificant was the incident that it had faded from memory almost as soon as it'd happened.

Lucas lay back on the bed despite the school nurse insisting he not lie down and closed his eyes. He never expected the kid to move so fast. Lucas hadn't even registered the kid had caught it, much less thrown it back, until he was staring at the ceiling with Ethan and Lance leaning over him, mouths hanging open.

The whispers had immediately begun to spread. People laughed. Someone in the stairwell said, "That's what you get." If Lucas ever found out who that little shit was, he'd pound his face into new and interesting shapes.

"Lucas? Are you feeling all right? Should you be lying down?"

Lucas cracked an eye to see Alicia standing over him looking concerned. He grinned a lazy crocodile smile. "Better now that I'm seeing you."

Alicia blushed and smiled back.

"We going out tonight, baby?"

"You know my dad won't let me go out during the week. This weekend for sure though."

"Come on," Lucas said, sliding a lazy finger up her leg. "Your pops loves me. He'll say yes."

Alicia stepped away from his finger before it moved into uncharted territory. "He doesn't like anyone enough to let me date on a school night."

Lucas sat up to pull her back over by the waist. "If you don't ask, you'll never know."

"I don't have to ask. I live with him."

"Yeah, but you don't know." Lucas let his hand drop down her back.

"Know what?" Mrs. Kelly strode back into the room.

Alicia took two quick steps away, cheeks burning red. Lucas remained silent, irritated with the interruption.

The nurse turned to Alicia. "Am I interrupting? Should I leave? Did you get your shot?"

"No, ma'am. Not interrupting. Yes, I got the shot," Alicia mumbled. Her cheeks flamed even brighter. Lucas grinned, enjoying her embarrassment.

"How about you leave Mr. Gahan alone? He needs to rest. Head injuries are a serious matter, even on a skull as thick as his. Head on back to class."

"Yes, ma'am." Alicia left the room without saying anything else to Lucas.

Mrs. Kelly turned her considerable bulk toward Lucas. "She's much too young for you. Four years is too far apart at your age. Don't lead that girl into trouble."

"How about you mind your business? Stop talking; my head hurts. And get me an ice pack." Lucas maintained eye contact with her, daring her to say something else. He'd date whoever he damn well pleased. Never mind what any fat school nurse thought about it. More than likely, she was mad she wasn't on the menu. Too old, too fat, too ugly, too bad.

"Boy, I don't care who your daddy is or what you do on the football field. You'll speak to me with respect."

"Whatever. Less talking, more getting my ice pack."

Knowing if she opened her mouth, she'd likely lose her job, Mrs. Kelly turned her back on the mouthy little prick. Whoever put the goose egg on Lucas's forehead deserved congratulations, and although she didn't say anything, she hoped his forehead hurt.

///

The first week back in school ended without further incident. Routines were established. Students memorized their classroom locations. Teachers launched into lessons after establishing class rules and handing out syllabi. Gossip spread of the freshman who'd knocked out Lucas Gahan in a stairwell. By the end of the week, the mystery around the anonymous freshman had grown. Rampant rumor suggested he was either a third-year freshman, on parole, a fearless drug dealer collecting a debt, a mixed martial arts fighter, a fugitive in the FBI witness relocation program, or possibly all the above.

Mark heard the stories and volunteered no information. Getting himself onto Lucas's radar wasn't something he planned on doing. Let them say what they wanted. Being a nobody held the occasional advantage. It was a lucky fluke, Mark decided. Karma coming back around. He bore the scars on his head from the last bottle and didn't plan on adding more. Let Lucas handle his business. Mark had his own concerns.

Alicia Foster studied herself in the mirror. *Not bad*, she thought. She could easily pass for sixteen, maybe even eighteen. Knowing her low-cut top exposing her budding cleavage wouldn't make it past her father, she covered up with a teal sweater, which matched her eyes. She'd ditch the sweater in Lucas's car after they were well away from her house.

The doorbell announced Lucas's arrival.

She stayed in the bathroom, waiting on her father to answer the door. Butterflies filled her stomach, and her knees wobbled. On every single Friday night before this one, she could be found playing on Dad's computer. They shared a World of Warcraft account.

She never thought she'd be dating a guy like Lucas. Or any guy, really. She was so awkward.

She'd been having lunch with her dad at Panda Express in the mall, and her dad had stepped off to the bathroom. Oblivious, she'd carried on eating her orange chicken until she noticed him standing beside her. Lucas was cool, confident, and spoke like they'd known each other for years. He'd been so casual about asking her out when she hadn't even known he knew she existed.

Lucas introduced himself when her father returned from the bathroom and clearly pretended not to notice the hostile looks he fired toward him. Smooth. Eventually, his confidence won over her father, and he got permission to take Alicia on a few day trips the last few weeks before school.

Even today, Dad still pretended not to like him.

She heard him making small talk with her father, "Good evening, Mr. Foster. Is Alicia ready?" She snuck a look down the stairs.

"No. She's upstairs getting ready. What time are you bringing her home?"

"The party will be over by midnight. Ethan's parents won't allow anyone to stay later."

"I want Alicia home by ten. And I don't mean 10:01. In this house by ten."

"Can do."

"Will there be drinking?"

"No, sir. Mr. Gilmore would never allow alcohol."

"The Gilmores are going to be there? I can call to make sure."

Lucas smiled his thousand-watt best. "Of course they'll be there. I'd never risk my spot on the team for some wild high school party. I have a future to think about." Lucas held up two fingers. "Scout's honor. This is more of a get-together to watch movies and eat pizza—that kind of thing. Totally innocent."

"Right."

Alicia could tell her father was working up to keeping her home. Her venture into dating had been hard on him. She went downstairs, interrupting the conversation before Dad gathered any momentum.

"Ready?" she asked Lucas.

Lucas turned his smile on her. "Sure am. You look amazing."

Alicia gave her dad a quick kiss on the cheek. "Bye, Daddy. Love you! See you!" She pulled Lucas out by the arm before her father found sufficient reason to keep his baby girl home.

Albert Foster next saw his daughter two days later, broken and in critical condition.

///

The day had started off so normal.

He'd woken up after two hours sleep, feeling refreshed as if he'd slept a full eight. After bounding down the stairs, he'd wolfed two bowls of cereal before his mother could make her toast, grunting answers at her attempts to engage him in conversation. He'd grabbed his backpack and popped out the door, hollering, "Bye, Mom! Love you!" before walking down their long gravel driveway into the morning fog.

Invigorated by the morning mist and feeling full of energy—which had nothing to do with the two bowls of Frosted Mini Wheats he'd inhaled—Mark had decided to jog to school. The jog became a run, and the run became a flat-out sprint.

Mark reveled in the sensation of motion, the exhilaration of speed he hadn't known he was capable of. His muscles pumped an easy rhythm his heart and lungs had no trouble fueling. His brain urged him to greater effort. Faster! Faster!

Caseknife Road slid by in a blur, becoming Commerce Street in downtown Summit Valley. Traffic picked up. Mark slid between cars, pedestrians, and bicycles on Commerce, sometimes with inches to spare, before hooking a left on Jefferson. The blocks flew past, and still he didn't tire. Mark felt he might run for days.

Past Jackson Park with its war memorial cannons hidden in the morning fog, past Chuck's on First, over the Memorial Bridge, and a few more steps saw him crossing Main Street ahead of a Summit Valley police cruiser Mark never saw.

Officer Roland shook his head. The kid was moving!

Main Street and the courthouse vanished unseen on Mark's right as he pushed his body to greater speed.

Tightening his backpack, Mark crossed Fourth and turned right on Fifth. He sprinted the rest of the route to school and stopped running only when he stepped onto school grounds. He'd run from his house to school—roughly four and a half miles as the crow flies—at a dead sprint, and he wasn't winded. He wasn't even sweating.

Mark felt no different than when he'd walked out the door this morning.

///

Mark couldn't stop thinking about his morning run. Not just his incredible stamina, which was growing by the day regardless of his diet or amount of exercise, but his agility too. This morning, he'd known exactly when to twist or leap to avoid an oncoming obstacle. He hadn't given it any conscious thought; his body had simply reacted when necessary. Much like when he'd caught the bottle, throwing it back before he could process the situation, his body dodged, leapt, and otherwise avoided dangers he couldn't even see in the morning fog.

His body moved to an internal radar Mark didn't understand, like a bat using echolocation, only Mark had no idea what was going on. But it felt good to move. Natural athletic ability was foreign to Mark. He wasn't an athlete. Sports weren't his thing unless camping counted as a sport. It didn't, did it?

Mark struggled to pay attention in Mr. Hagen's biology, his last class for the day. Next came the weekend. Mark didn't have any particular plan, other than to run Caseknife Road from Commerce back to the dam and see how long it took him to get tired. Maybe he could fashion his newfound energy into a way to help Mom make some extra money.

Mark's leg vibrated. He needed to know what his new limits were. Running over four miles at a dead sprint in thick autumn fog and early morning school traffic should have left him exhausted.

A deep exasperation from not being outside set in. He craved his feet gliding over pavement, barely touching the earth, propelling him forward. Breath steady in his lungs, heartbeat strong in his chest, wind cool on his forehead as it brushed hair back from his brow, arms pumping in time. Instead, he was stuck in a darkened classroom watching some awful droning film on cell division—

Riiiipppp.

Mark leaned over and saw the toes on his right foot had thickened and elongated. The ripping sound he'd heard was gleaming eight-inch silver claws blasting the rubber toe of his shoe free of the canvas. Hiding his foot underneath his backpack before anyone could see, Mark said a silent grateful prayer the room was dark and his desk was in the back by the door. Panic rose in his chest on fluttery wings. Everyone had to be staring. He looked around.

Students sat in neat rows fighting sleep, bored disinterest on most faces. Two small sources of light drew Mark's eye—one from the hallway, which spilled through a small rectangular window in the door, the other from a small lamp on Mr. Hagen's desk that illuminated a tiny circle for him to grade papers or read. The miracle of mitosis had lost its charm for Mr. Hagen.

Mark rolled the now detached tip of his Converse under his foot, flexing his strange new toes. The claws dug easily through the laminate tile and into the concrete beneath without leaving a blemish on the mirror shine. The narration on the film masked the slight grinding noise his foot made when digging into the floor.

Mark sat up straight, covered in a nervous sweat. Four deep grooves now marred the floor beneath the desk in front of him. When the lights came up, it was going to be obvious something had happened here. He needed to leave. Now. Anywhere else would be better.

Mark rolled the toe of his Converse, connected only by the sole, back and forth underneath his foot. He stood, trying his best to hide his foot with his backpack, and mumbled the word "bathroom" to Mr. Hagen, quickly backing out the door. Mr. Hagen grunted a response.

The hallway was blessedly free of people and class time quiet. Other than a slight itch, his foot felt fine, like it always did. Like his foot. Though being so much longer than the other foot, it made walking difficult. The ruined end of his shoe flopping around didn't help either.

Once in the bathroom, Mark locked himself in a stall. His problem was worse than he initially thought. In addition to the claws on his toes, another shorter but thicker claw had grown from his heel, ripping through sock and shoe. Despite his best efforts, his new appendages had dug into the tile all the way down the hall, into the bathroom, and into the stall. At the time, he hadn't noticed the stubby one on his heel and had focused only on keeping his toes away from the ground.

Now a fine trail dug into the concrete and led right to the stall he was currently hiding in. As soon as the bell rang or an administrator walked down the hall or a teacher noticed or anyone with functional eyesight saw, they would be led directly to him. And Mark wasn't running anywhere with one giant clown foot.

He needed to get his ruined shoe off to minimize further damage to his mangled Converse. Then he'd start working on a way to get out of this mess. He'd leave and go home, one shoe be damned. Sticking to backyards, parks, and woods, Mark knew how to make it home without ever crossing a single street, thus keeping his potential exposure to a minimum. If he got home without being seen, he'd have the weekend to wait for his foot to shrink back to normal. If it wasn't better by Monday, he'd worry about it then.

For now, he had to get out of there. And that meant getting the shoe off.

"Having some trouble there, son?"

Einar!

"Einar!" Mark jerked the stall door open. "I'd almost convinced myself it wasn't real!"

"And that?" Einar nodded toward Mark's clawed foot. "That real?"

"What's happening to me?"

Arms folded, Einar leaned against the sink with his beat-up cowboy hat riding low and shining belt buckle riding high, appearing for all the world like he had business in the second-floor bathroom of Summit Valley High School. Perfectly natural for him to be there, in this place, at this time.

"Where have you been? Where did you come from?" Mark asked.

Einar ignored both questions.

"You really don't have much time here, Mark, so let's save the explanations for when we can have us a sit-down."

Mark nodded.

"You can fix that if you want to." Again, Einar nodded at Mark's foot.

"What? How?"

"Pull them back."

Mark narrowed his eyes. "Huh? How do I do that?"

"You extended the claws. Kind of a dumb thing to do in the middle of biology class. Now retract them."

"Just like that?"

"Just like that."

"Einar, that doesn't help. If I could do that, I would have by now."

"That's all the help you need. You control the power. It doesn't control you."

Mark closed his eyes, imagining his feet—his normal feet. No claws. No thick scaly black toes. No claw on the heel.

Was that a tingling sensation?

He peeked down. Nope. Still had claws.

Einar stood, eyebrows raised. "Anytime." He tapped his wrist with a forefinger.

Mark tried again. This time, he imagined the claws pulling back into the flesh of his feet inch by inch. A sudden pain dropped him back onto the commode. Mark gritted his teeth, grabbing his right calf. Fire ants were chewing on his feet. Flaming fire ants. With chainsaws. Had to be.

When he opened his eyes again, Mark saw only his foot. No claws. And Einar was gone.

Mark stood, gingerly testing his weight on his right foot. Now that he was able to think clearly, it dawned on him that Einar hadn't casted a reflection while leaning against the sink in front of the mirrors. No reflection at all.

Making his way home turned out to be the least eventful part of the day. Maintaining a westerly direction through open backyards on Fifth Street, Mark gradually turned south, crossed Peak Creek, and began the long climb through the mountains toward his house. Loose twigs occasionally poked through the gaping holes in his shoe, but all things considered, the Converse held up remarkably well. It would make quite an endorsement if the situation weren't so bizarre. Converse: tough as they come and withstands it all—even dragon foot!

Mark checked his Warcraft account. Alicia hadn't been at school today. She wasn't online either. Currently the larger concern was repairing the blown-out end of his Converse. Luckily, the old canvas had ripped along the edge of the rubber toe. He expected his mother to go completely sideways when she found out. New shoes weren't cheap.

Once a year, before school, they went shoe shopping. The old pair—if they still fit—Mark kept for cutting grass and general messing around after school. No such luck this year; his feet had grown two full sizes. The Converse were the only pair he owned, and they couldn't afford another pair.

Frowning at his dirty toes, Mark found small comfort in the thought. It wasn't his fault. That didn't make this any less of his problem to deal with though. His sock was ruined too, stained with road grit underneath a shredded rubber ruin. *Nevermind the socks, I can hide those.*

Having ditched early, he'd made it home before Mom with plenty of time to spare. Feeling a mix of guilt and exhilaration, wondering if the school would contact his mother, Mark went to grab some duct tape and a pair of scissors.

He tore off four six-inch strips and carefully overlapped the edges to make a small six-inch square sheet of duct tape. Then he tore off another four strips to make another sheet. Pressing the sticky sides together, Mark made a two-ply patch of duct tape large enough to cover the hole in the heel of his shoe. He slid the patch in on the inside, then used another strip of duct tape to hold the patch in place.

On the outside, the hole in the heel remained obvious, but Mark had a plan. He used to build Gundams with his father – big plastic robots. After Dad died, building models wasn't much fun, though he couldn't bring himself to throw the stuff away. He wouldn't let his mother throw it out either, not that she really tried; she missed Dad as bad as Mark did.

He removed a dual compound epoxy, black and silver acrylic paints, and a few brushes. After mixing the epoxy, which was a little stiff on top from sitting in the closet, Mark filled the hole in careful even layers until flush with the rest of the heel. He brushed black paint into the epoxy to darken it to a similar color of the surrounding black canvas. Then he set the shoe in a vise on his desk to dry.

While waiting on the epoxy to dry, Mark mixed another batch. He loosely reattached the toe with a piece of duct tape—just enough to hold the rubber in place—then sealed the rip with the fresh batch of epoxy. It took a thick application without an underlying patch for the epoxy to bond with, and in the end, Mark thought he might end up filing the inside of his shoe to prevent blisters. With any luck, the makeshift seals wouldn't hinder the natural movement of his foot. Time would tell.

Mark opened a window to thin the chemical fumes and sat on his bed. Had this day really happened? His busted shoe was proof it had. What was going on here?

Following an urge, he got back up and, using the silver paint, painted a design on the drying heel. A small graphic, a doodle. Meaningless, really. It could've been an arrow or a shooting star or a dragon rising on folded wing.

///

Boy'd messed up again. Wayne wondered not for the first time—not even the first time today—if he would've been better off drowning the boy as a baby. The Lord saw fit to bless him with the one son and at the cost of his Julia. It was a trade Wayne found a bit unfair at times. He loved the boy, but Lord A'mighty , Lucas was a champion fuck-up. World class.

Led around by the pecker—most bucks at his age were—he needed firm hands, guidance, and discipline, yet Lucas had never understood the meaning of the word no. Sure, Wayne was partly to blame. He spoiled the boy. He was the last link to his only love, after all.

Sure as the sunrise, Lucas could be counted on to mess up. Wayne, on the other hand, handled business. His personal hero, Elvis Presley, had coined the term TCB: Taking Care of Business. Wayne liked that. Wayne took care of business. Adapting this to his own personal mantra, Wayne shortened it to HB: Handling Business.

Always willing to go the extra mile, get up earlier, stay later, work harder—that was Wayne. And if he happened to undercut someone, backstab the occasional friend or coworker, make a dirty deal now and then, well, it was all a part of handling business. No one mattered more than number one. Julia had understood that.

She'd helped him elevate his game to the big time. Thanks to her, he was someone in this town. Wayne Gahan owned Summit Valley Motors, a large respectable chain in the New River Valley and a monopoly on the car market. Julia had diversified their assets into various real estate ventures in the area. She'd had vision, and now Wayne maintained the fortune she'd helped him build. Without her, the dynasty wouldn't expand.

Lucas, more Wayne than Julia, made a better Fredo than Don Corleone. The boy lacked the flair of his mother or the cunning of his father. He'd come home last Friday covered in blood—again—telling Wayne he'd done it again. Wayne waited until the string bean had been found before making this trip. First, Wayne handled Lucas's business.

Lucas would go on to a good school, play some college ball, and then take over for his old man, and until then, Wayne would make sure Lucas didn't throw his future away for some silly slit. And if Lucas needed the occasional reminder of who the big bull was, Wayne would be happy to help. Spare the rod, spoil the child.

Children never appreciate the sacrifices a parent makes.

Behind the wheel of his Cadillac—Elvis loved a Caddy—Wayne hummed along with the radio. Toby Keith proudly proclaimed he was an American soldier. Wayne had never served—he had a criminal record—yet he still felt a swelling of pride and wiped a tear away.

Yes, God was good. He'd get Lucas on the straight and narrow. And he was damn proud to be an American.

Albert Foster sat by his daughter's bed at Summit Valley Hospital. Alicia drifted in and out of consciousness as she had for most of the week while the police filed in and out and conducted their quiet interviews. Gentle stares had alternated between sympathetic and accusatory until they'd verified Albert's whereabouts. It was one of the only times in his life he'd felt relief for needing to work overtime. According to the police, he couldn't be the monster who'd raped and beat his daughter nearly to death.

Of course, Albert already knew where the blame lay. Lucas Gahan. And he'd told the detectives as much. He didn't understand why they continued to question him. Alicia had told them Lucas did this to her. What more did they need?

Right now, there were no police. No questions. Only a father nursing his wounded daughter, holding her hand, willing her some type of peace. Praying to ease a suffering he couldn't comprehend from wounds far deeper than the physical. Tears to the soul, scarring in the mind, broken trust, fear, self-loathing, and pits potentially too deep, too viscous to crawl out of.

Alicia's heart rate and blood pressure monitor hummed, beeping rhythmically, content in her progress. Her vitals were strong. Physically, she was a healthy young woman despite her trauma. Albert maintained faith she'd bounce back. He'd never seen anything beyond his baby girl. She deserved better than a janitor for a father, but he was what she had, and no one loved her more. The things she could do on a computer! And her grades! Already in college programs as a freshman in high school. Alicia had a future if she didn't let that animal take it away from her.

She'd show him. She was better than Lucas and better than this town.

A tear—another soldier from an army of heartbreak—ran along the gummy tracks of its predecessors, following gravity's mandate from the corner of Albert's eye to the tile beside Alicia's bed.

A knock at the door startled him. Wiping his eyes, Albert attempted to focus on his visitor. Wayne Gahan stuck his head in the door. A spike of fear wormed through Albert's guts, then burned out in a white-hot flame of anger. The arrogance. The absolute gall. The balls!

"Now, I know it's not a good time..." Wayne stood in the doorway holding up a soothing hand. In the other, he held a bouquet of flowers with an assortment of star-shaped foil balloons of varying sizes and colors. A large star in the middle trailed a rainbow with the words Get Well Soon! printed in cartoony font. All the stars wore doofy, vapid smiles. "But I felt it the Christian thing to come check on her condition."

"Did you teach your boy it was the Christian thing to beat and rape young women?" Albert rose to his feet, hands in tight fists at his sides. The balloons bobbed merrily.

"Well, no. Mr. Foster, I—well, I understand your anger—"

"Do you?" Albert took a step, dark circles underneath his eyes, face flushed in rage. "I bet Alicia feels better knowing you understand as she lies here in the hospital, where your son put her. After he raped her."

Wayne backed a half step into the hall, rodent-like eyes scanning a quick left-right, nose twitching, like he scented danger. "Mr. Foster, you're upset. What father wouldn't be?" Wayne continued backing into the hall, angling himself toward the nurses' station. "But my Lucas is a good boy. A little wild sometimes, but he's a got a good heart." Wayne spoke fast, seemingly knowing there were only seconds left before Albert Foster lost the little self-control he possessed, possibly laying him out in a bed in this same hospital. "We both feel awful about poor Alicia—"

"Don't you say her name! Don't you dare!" Albert hissed.

"Which is why," Wayne continued, as if he'd never been interrupted, "I've paid all of her present hospital expenses and left a blank check for all future medical costs associated with this...incident. All rehabilitation, therapy, psychiatric treatment—the whole shebang, Mr. Foster. Of course, if you assault me..." Wayne let the sentence hang.

Three nurses, the on-call doctor, and a security guard gathered at the nurses' station, watching the confrontation. The security guard set down the cup of coffee he'd been working on and left through a set of double doors, keys jingling with his departure. No one else moved.

Albert stopped advancing. "You're trying to, what? Buy me off?"

"Of course not. A bribe implies my son committed a crime."

"He's a rapist. That's a crime. I intend to see he spends the next twenty years in prison getting daily what he gave to my daughter."

"Careful with the R word. Lucas has a bright future ahead of him in college, where Julia intended. My boy ain't headed to prison. I brought something. The police report. Toxicology. Results from the initial exam."

"I don't believe a word you say." Albert's hands hung loose at his sides, trembling. His nose already crusted with snot, his bloodshot eyes teared up again.

"Mr. Foster—Albert—I don't blame you one bit. You don't need to believe me. I only ask, as one father to another, that you listen to me. I'm here for you. Yes, I'm here to protect my boy, but I'm here to protect Alicia too." Wayne gestured to a pair of stiff pleather hospital chairs outside Alicia's room. The police had sat out there after Alicia had first been brought to this room, after the exams and intrusive questions.

Albert thought again about their accusatory stares. God, he was exhausted. Never in his life had he ever felt so deeply bone weary. Albert felt tired in his soul. All he wanted in the world was to take his daughter home and listen to her play on the computer while he caught the 'skins game on TV. They'd order a pizza from Domino's along with one of those cookie-brownie combo dessert things she loved and drink Mountain Dew. She'd be safe, not raped, beaten, and in a hospital, and there wouldn't be any police with their damning stares. Best of all, there'd be no Wayne with his greasy sympathy.

Albert sat.

Wayne slid into the seat next to him, the observation window into Alicia's room at their backs. The hiss and beep of Alicia's monitoring equipment was still audible over the chaotic hush of the hallway. Phony concern oozed off Wayne. While comical under other circumstances, Wayne's used car salesman sincerity grated on Albert's frayed nerves.

Wayne's brow furrowed in what Albert was sure he thought of as fraternal sympathy. A couple of regular Joes, doing our best to handle our wayward children, the look said. Brothers in fatherhood united in tragedy. From his suit pocket, Wayne removed a thick packet of folded papers. "The reports I mentioned. Lucas isn't responsible for Alicia's unfortunate condition."

"What?"

"I'm sorry. I know you're looking for someone to blame, but it's true. Lucas didn't do it."

"You're lying."

" Albert"—Wayne leaned in, his breath stank of Wrigley's Spearmint—"if we have to go to court, this will not go your way. I have witness statements from thirteen boys at the party stating your daughter conducted herself in a lewd and lascivious manner."

"What does that mean?"

"She danced naked for the boys. Then had sex with them one at a time. Each time she came out of the bedroom, she announced she needed a 'real man.'"

"That's a lie."

"Her blood toxicology shows she was out of her mind on alcohol, marijuana, and MDMA—or ecstasy, E, Molly, whatever the kids are calling it now."

"My daughter is not a drug-addicted whore."

"And my son wouldn't keep the company of one. I'm saying nothing of the kind. Alicia has been to my home, Mr. Foster. I know she's a good girl. But sometimes kids experiment, and things can get out of hand. Kids get wild. Don't forget what it's like to be young." Wayne nodded his head. He really did look sympathetic...

Albert started to wonder if Wayne might be right. Maybe Alicia got herself caught up in a wild night. Things spiraled beyond her control.

"Lucas said he dropped her off at home, but then he told me he lied. Truth is, Lucas, Alicia, Ethan, and Lance went for food at the truck stop off I-81 near Fort Chiswell. You know the one?"

Albert did. Alicia was found in the trash and weeds in the lot behind the truck stop, bloody and naked. The trucker who found her thought he'd found a dead body. When he realized Alicia was still breathing, he'd covered her nakedness with his flannel, then left after giving the state patrol a statement without collecting his jacket. The police told Albert the trucker had cried for the little girl he'd found. They didn't tell him the trucker's name. The flannel hung on the back of Alicia's hospital door.

"Lucas said he went to the bathroom, and when he got back, Alicia was gone. Ethan and Lance said she saw a 'real man' and went outside. They didn't see who she was talking about and didn't follow her. When Lucas came back from the bathroom, he made them get up, and the three of them tried to find her without success. Eventually, they got scared and came home. Lucas said he thought maybe she caught a ride with a trucker. He said she was pretty messed up. Look, Albert, I take no pleasure in telling you about this. My boy is responsible for poor choices, drug use, but not rape. Not violence. He was stupid, and maybe cowardly, but he isn't a rapist."

"According to this story, he abandoned her—a fourteen-year-old girl—when she was out of her mind," Albert said, head in his hands.

Wayne rubbed his back. "Which is why I'm here. To take responsibility for our part in this terrible chain of events. Responsibility anywhere along the way might have prevented all of this. It's a goddamn shame all the way around. Do I need to mention I play golf with the district attorney? We've spoken about this at length. He isn't going to pursue charges. Now, if we go to court, all of this will come out, but we aren't going to court. Lucas won't go to prison. Neither will his friends or any of those boys at the party. You know it. I know it. Things work different when you have money."

"Laws for thee, but not for me," Albert whispered.

"One way to put it, I suppose. I'm not a crude man. Flaunting is crude, and my Julia wouldn't have stood for it. I'm a realist. Alicia's life would be ruined. She'd never recover, not here. Word would get out about that night. People talk. You know how it is. I want to protect her as much as I want to protect Lucas. I see no need to put our business out in the public eye. Let me pay for the medical bills, therapy, whatever treatment she may need, quietly, in private. Let her maintain her dignity."

Albert broke down, crying into his hands. "You work your whole life to provide for them, protect them."

"Brother, I know. That's exactly what we're going to do. Protect them both. Come on by the dealership sometime, and I'll personally see to it you get something special. Now, if you'll sign right here."

///

Nicole Little, RN and Amber Venters, LPN leaned against the desk watching the two men. Dr. Rustvold waited to start his rounds until he was sure the pair weren't going to fight. Adrian Johnson, the other LPN on shift, left with Dr. Rustvold. Nicole was sure Adrian was fucking the doc—or at least trying to.

Security had left when it looked like Wayne Gahan might get his ass beat. Matt said he couldn't be around to break that up. Gahan had burned him on a Ford Expedition, charging $12,000 over the manufacturer suggested retail price and financing it at a whopping 27 percent interest. The truck broke down three months after driving it off the lot and ended up being nothing but a headache. He'd never buy another vehicle from Gahan and left the scene with the hope that Mr. Foster beat Gahan until they couldn't see him anymore, then beat where they saw him last.

They sure didn't look like they felt like fighting now. They looked like best friends—Albert crying, Wayne consoling.

Amber leaned in close. "Can you believe this happy crappy?"

"Not really," Nicole said.

"His kid"—Amber nodded at Wayne— "puts his in here. Raped her! And they're acting like besties!"

"Gahan is a snake. Worms his way out of everything. I heard this isn't the first time either."

"First time for what?" Amber asked.

"First time his kid's done something like this."

"Girl, you're lying!"

"Swear I'm not!"

"Why haven't I heard this before?"

"'Cause every time he does something, his daddy swoops in, throws money everywhere, and everyone forgets." Nicole shook her head.

"Except the victims."

"Yeah. Except them."

"I wish we could hear what they're talking about," Amber whispered.

"It's not hard to figure out. He's convincing Mr. Foster not to pursue charges, like he has any say in the matter. Somehow, he's got him believing Alicia brought it on herself. No charges will come from this. Wait and see." She blew out a breath. "That guy is a greasy shit after a shower. He ruins everything. I'm going back to work."

Years of discipline, grifting, confidence gaming, and politics kept the gigantic smile from Wayne's face as Albert Foster signed the paperwork releasing Lucas from blame in exchange for the Gahan covering his brat's medical expenses. Lucas had dodged another bullet—with ol' Daddy's help, of course. Always with Wayne's help.

Tucking the papers back into his inner jacket pocket, Wayne made his way to the elevator. A young nurse—pretty in a country way—nodded politely as she went about her business pushing a cart loaded with medical supplies. The name tag on her breast read AMBER.

A little dumpy, but I'd fuck her and not tell anyone about it. Wayne nodded and smiled enough to be polite.

As he stepped off the elevator, he took the "evidence" out of his pocket and dropped it in the trash on the way out the door. The two-month-old sales reports had served their purpose.

///

Albert sat in the hall for a moment longer after Wayne left. The bills were going to be paid; that was a relief. Also, they might get a new car out of this deal. It wasn't a complete loss. But Alicia—what was he going to do about Alicia? Where had this come from? Rebelliousness wasn't in her nature.

Standing, Albert decided not to ask his daughter about it until she felt better. The hospital—especially when recovering from a savage attack—wasn't the time or place for an interrogation. Love and support were what Alicia needed from her father right now. Assured in this proper course, Albert stepped into the room to find Alicia sitting up, tears streaming down her face.

"You believe him, don't you?"

///

The shoe held up better than Mark had dared to hope. The epoxy holding the toes together hadn't bothered his feet at all. His mother noticed the custom paint, complimenting him on his artistry and asking when he planned on releasing his own line that would put Nike out of business. Ha-ha.

Mark's concerns lay a long way from the busted Converse on his feet. His mom was worried about money again. Trying to hide it made things around the house tense. She became irritable and snapped at Mark over little things. Bone chose safer sleeping grounds in Mark's bedroom instead of underneath the kitchen table, and he always slipped out when voices rose. After complimenting him on his shoes, his mom reamed him over not taking the garbage out.

Mark mumbled, "Yes, ma'am," and hustled through the house gathering trash. With his newfound energy, it took no time at all.

Mark completed his assigned chore while Mom scowled at the bill from Appalachian Power they'd be sixty dollars short on this month.

"Did you get that trash out?" she asked.

"Yes, ma'am. Sure did."

"All of it?"

"Hey, I'm good like that!"

"If I go check?"

"You'll see what an amazing son you have." Mark offered his most charming smile.

"It's a good thing I like you." She rolled her eyes. "What do you want to do for dinner, amazing son of mine?"

"What do we have?"

"I could fry us up a couple of burgers. Or we might have stuff for spaghetti."

"What's easier?"

"Burgers."

"Burgers, then," Mark said.

"You're a good boy. I'm sorry I snapped at you."

"No problem, Mom. I love you. I know you're worried about the bills. It's not me you're mad at."

"How'd you get so smart, huh?"

"I got it from Dad."

Her eyes narrowed. "Mark, honey?"

"Yes, Mom?"

"Get out of my kitchen."

///

Mark went upstairs to his room to wait for dinner. Thinking about his feet and the claws hidden within got him wondering. Could he do that with his hands? *What else can I do?* Einar had said he controlled the power. It didn't control him.

Reptile.

What else?

Mark held his right hand up, willing something to happen. Anything. Scales. Claws.

Nothing.

Closing his eyes, Mark envisioned bright silver claws bursting from his fingertips and growing longer, sharper, like polished silver. He imagined his knuckles thickening, covered in rough black scales. His hands became muscular, strong, capable of ripping through cinder block without marring the shine of the claws. Mark opened his eyes.

Nothing.

His shoulders tired from holding his normal hands out in front of him. There was a trick here, and Mark was going to figure it out.

"Mark! Dinner!" Mom called from downstairs.

Thing was, he knew dinner had finished cooking ten minutes ago. She'd plated everything, went to her bedroom, and locked the door before crying into her pillow. Mark heard her sobbing and could smelled the facial soap she'd used all the way from his room.

Mark had a plan to help.

Mitch "Millie" Drummond looked up from his phone as the boy walked in. Millie, a permanent fixture at the warehouse for National Linen, had worked the counter since the late 1970s. In that time, he'd worked up to manager, but his preferred post was still the one he'd started in all those years ago—the counter. Millie was a people person. He loved to gossip and always had a word for the local restauranteurs, suppliers, or folks working in hospitality.

Hospitals, retirement homes, catering businesses, cafés, B and Bs, flower shops, retail stores, and anyone else who wanted or needed good quality linen in the Summit Valley area knew Millie. He'd taken orders for weddings, funerals, business lunches, and everything in between, but never in that time had he had a request like the one before him.

This underage pipsqueak, no bigger than a minute, wanted a job.

He wanted cash. Daily. Off the books. And he claimed he'd outwork the best guys Millie had.

"You can keep them on—you know, for taxes or whatever. Keep things looking legit. But you aren't going to need them," he said.

"Is that right?" Millie didn't know if he should humor the kid or throw him out on his ass. The boy had hustle, and Millie respected the stones on the little guy.

Mark squared his shoulders. "You don't have to take my word for it. Give me five minutes. I can move whatever you need wherever you need it to go faster than anyone else you have. If not, kick me out, and I'll never bother you again. What do you have to lose?"

Millie grunted. "Hmm. Okay, kid. Let's go have a laugh. Follow me."

Mark grinned and followed Millie into the warehouse. Millie was in his sixties, with short gray hair over ice blue eyes that had faded a bit over the years. Millie looked like a seasoned drinker, and years of exposure to harsh detergents and chlorine bleaches had left his eyes red and rheumy. Yellowed leathery skin stretched taut over years of muscles grown hard throwing heavy bundles of laundry.

Millie's rough exterior belied a kinder heart. He loved to talk and joke, and he didn't know what kind of raw deal sent a young'un into a place like this looking for work, but if he could push a broom around,

Millie planned on helping the kid out. Better in here than out on the street selling drugs or some such. You heard about it on the news all the time. Sad old world.

They made their way through racks of clean folded linen that stretched to the ceiling twenty feet up. The kid's head twitch back and forth at the variety. People never failed to be surprised at the immensity of the warehouse.

Yesterday, Robert pulled ten stacks of fifty single sheets, ten stacks of fifty fitted sheets, ten stacks of fifty draw sheets, ten stacks of knit fitted sheets, and ten stacks of fifty standard 42-by-34-inch pillowcases in preparation for the weekly delivery to Summit Valley Community Hospital. Two hundred and fifty pounds of clean medical grade packaged linen bundled on the floor awaited transfer to a pallet.

"See the stack of pallets by the wall?"

"Yes, sir."

"Bring one over here."

Mark ran over, flipped a pallet off the top, and ran it back. He set it on the floor in front of Millie.

"Christ, boy! I'd a never thought you'd move like that! Let's see if you can do it with those stacks of sheets. Careful, they're heavy!"

Mark grabbed a bundle in each hand and stacked one on each corner of the pallet. Then he grabbed another pallet and stacked twenty-five bundles on the first pallet, twenty-five on the second.

"Done!" Mark turned, smiling at Millie.

"Son, you aren't even out of breath." Millie had never seen anything like it. The kid moved like his feet were on fire.

"I know," he said.

"That took you ninety seconds."

"It was my first time. I'll be faster when I know what I'm doing."

"That job was slated for Robert."

"Pay me half of what you'd pay him to do it this afternoon."

Millie narrowed his eyes. "Tell me why you're here."

"My mom and I need money."

"Where's your dad?"

"Dead."

"I'm sorry to hear that. What happened?"

"He was a soldier," Mark said.

Millie nodded. "Understand I can't pay you what you're worth."

"Yeah." Mark nodded.

"But I'll do better than half of what I give those jokers. Can you work after hours? Early in the morning or late at night?"

"Yeah. I can do either. I come by here on my way to school. I live on Caseknife."

"Okay, good. Me too. You the Branton boy?"

"Mark."

"Mark, I knew your daddy." Millie stuck out his hand. "My name's Millie. Lemme go get you something to load this up."

Mark ran home sporting a wide grin. He'd worked a couple of minutes and made a hundred dollars. Not bad for a Saturday afternoon. And Millie had asked him to come back! He had a job! Moving linen was easy—if boring—work, and Mama was going to love the extra money.

Bursting in the door, he called out, "Mom! Where are you!"

"In the kitchen!"

Mark's mother was in her usual spot at the kitchen table, bills spread out in front of her.

"Whatcha doing?" Mark asked.

"Trying to figure out how to pay these damn bills. Same ol' same."

"Would this help?" Mark dropped five twenties in front of her.

"Where did you get this?"

"I got a job."

"You got a what? Where did you get a job?"

"Oh, it's no big deal. I've been pushing a broom around National Linen after school and on the occasional weekend. Millie is a good guy, and he pays me in cash." Mark felt bad for the lie, but sometimes a little lie wasn't so bad. Mom didn't need to know *everything*.

"Is that all you do?"

"I mop too."

"Is that where you've been going on the weekends?"

"Usually. I wanted to surprise you. I know we need the money."

She looked at the cash. "What did I ever do to deserve a son like you?" That stung. But her smile—her smile made the white lie perfectly acceptable, right?

///

Mark heard about Alicia not from anyone at school or from Alicia herself. He overheard Millie gossiping with the guy who delivered the weekly linen supply to Summit Valley Community Hospital. Mark sat at the counter pretending to be Millie's grandson for customers, learning the register, and spending a large amount of time playing Tetris on Millie's ancient but beloved Game Boy.

The driver, Steve, dated a nurse named Nicole whom he called Nikki—Nikki said this, Nikki did that, Nikki, Nikki, Nikki. She worked a trauma unit, and Steve put the respect on her name. Mark had almost tuned Steve out—he was kind of boring—when he mentioned that Nikki had witnessed Wayne Gahan blackmail a rape victim's father.

Millie asked who the father was. Steve didn't know. A janitor or something.

Alicia's father worked as a janitor at Summit Valley High School, and Mark hadn't seen him or Alicia in a couple of weeks. Alicia also hadn't been online since she went on her date with Lucas.

Mark had no trouble believing Lucas capable of rape. Lucas was an animal.

Millie wished Steve well and said they'd see him next week.

"Hey, kid, feeling okay? Moving those sheets catching up to you?"

"No. I'm fine." Mark turned the Game Boy off. "Millie, mind if I leave?"

"You've taken care of everyone's work for the weekend. I guess you don't have to sit at the counter if you don't want to. I'll tell everyone you wanted to go home. You're looking a little pale, kid. Get some rest, and I'll see you Wednesday evening, if you don't mind?"

"I can make Wednesday. Thanks, Millie."

"Let me get your envelope. I gave you a bonus." Millie wandered back between the stacks in his slow meandering way, returning a few minutes later with an envelope bearing Mark's name. "You've put out more work for me in three weeks than some of these other jokers have in six months. You deserve this."

Mark folded the envelope and stuffed it into his front pocket without opening it. He needed to think. "Thanks again, Millie. See ya."

///

Millie grunted, holding the door for Mark. Kid worked like a demon and for the most part was a good boy, but there was something about him. Something...dangerous.

///

Turning left, Mark headed for Third Street. The remains of Summit Valley Furniture Plant loomed on his left, a multi-floored ghost of better times. Mark glanced at the clock tower over the courthouse to his right—not quite seven in the morning. The whole weekend stretched out in front of him.

Summit Valley remained Saturday morning sleepy. Few cars and virtually no other pedestrians haunted the streets this early. Mark had gone in to work at four thirty and finished the list Millie had for him by quarter after five. After that, he'd sat at the counter playing Tetris while Millie supervised the industrial pickups. Most of those were gone by six.

A sudden revving startled Mark, and a Mustang crossed the intersection at Third before Mark got there. The driver gunned the engine as the sports car cleared the intersection and leapt ahead with a burst of speed. From the corner, Mark looked after the familiar red car as it disappeared around the corner of Third and Jefferson, then saw why the driver had accelerated.

Lucas had accelerated to hit a bird that had landed in the street. Mark walked over to the struggling bird—a sparrow investigating a piece of popcorn. Blood leaked from the bird's mouth. Its body was misshapen, lumpy, and it held one wing at a strange angle. Mark guessed several bones were broken. The little guy must've been in a tremendous amount of pain.

After removing the gloves he wore to protect himself from pallet splinters, Mark scooped the wounded sparrow from the road as gently as possible. Cupping the creature's broken body in his left hand, he cupped his right over the top, forming a fleshy cocoon with the bird tucked inside. Mark scooted over to the sidewalk, careful not to jostle his wounded cargo.

Kneeling on the curb, Mark followed an impulse and began to gingerly feel the bird in his hands. Closing his eyes, Mark imagined broken bones knitting together, ruptured organs healing, snapped feathers mending. The tips of Mark's fingers sprouted silver claws, extending four inches before withdrawing back into his fingers. Blood dripped from the tips and into the gutter. Mark's eyes blazed with fiery red light beneath his eyelids.

An onlooker might've thought him sick—hands clutched to his chest, eyes closed, kneeling half on the sidewalk, half in the gutter. If you had walked up to him to ask if he felt okay, you'd have felt the heat radiating off him. You'd have wondered if he had a fever. And then if it was it contagious. Then you'd have noticed the bloody fingertips. Or maybe you'd have heard the deep bass growling coming from somewhere within his impossibly thin throat. Any onlooker would have been alarmed by the sight of Mark before hurrying along about their own business and away from the strange young man on the street.

In his mind's eye, Mark experienced the sparrow's hunger, its curiosity at spotting the popcorn kernel. Then the spike of panic as a great roaring beast charged.

Run! Fly!

Not fast enough.

Hard crunch and pain unlike anything ever known. Careening uncontrolled through the air. Falling. The beast still roaring but farther away, farther now.

Pain. Wings don't work. Can't move. Blood. His blood. Blood on the food. Not hungry anymore. Shadows closing in. Acceptance.

Pain chases the shadows back. Warm. No pain. Light. Light bringer.

Mark's forearms pulsed with tiny flashes following a path to his palms.

Then he opened his eyes, breathing hard.

Opening his hands, he smiled. The sparrow stood upright on his palm, whole. After chirping once, it flew off to attend to whatever business it had before being hit by Lucas's Mustang. Mark watched it go before pushing to his feet and staggering, then threw up into a trash can. The Hardee's sausage biscuit with mustard and orange juice Millie had brought for breakfast this morning tasted better the first time around. Wiping his mouth, Mark looked around to see if anyone had seen him revive the bird, then puke his guts out. He never noticed the blood in the gutter.

Downtown traffic began to pick up as Mark walked down Third Street. No foot traffic passed him, although clerks, court workers, bailiffs, jailors, lawyers, and small-town politicians—the literal cogs of the machine of government—began filling the parking lot next to the courthouse and filing through the doors in ones and twos, their morning coffee caressing the air with fragrant steam.

Helping the sparrow took more out of him than he'd realized. For the first time in months, Mark felt tired, though his weariness felt closer to an athlete after a good workout. A healthy tired.

Following a rumpled suit into the courthouse proper, Mark was stopped by an overweight sheriff's deputy in a brown uniform. The suit stepped around the security, continuing on unmolested. Mark was forced to empty his pockets, step through a metal detector, and stand in place while the deputy ran a wand over his body, searching for whatever the metal detector might have missed. Mark wasn't carrying any metal. Or a cell phone. Or a weapon of mass destruction in his back pocket.

Once the fat deputy felt assured fourteen-year-old Mark had no plans of wreaking havoc on the courthouse, he grudgingly allowed him to pass. During his inspection, several people had walked through the metal detector and retrieved their belongings from the fat deputy's equally fat partner without further inspection. Had to be sure they kept those unruly teenagers from running amok in public spaces and knew who was boss. Or maybe it was because Mark was poor and looked it.

Not to be intimidated, Mark asked, "Excuse me, is there somewhere I can go to get information?"

The deputy grunted. The sound, remarkably piglike, forced Mark to stifle a giggle. "Information about what?"

"I have a friend who got hurt in a crime. I'm wondering what she can do."

"Call a cop."

"Hopefully she'd find someone as helpful, sympathetic, and friendly as you." Mark smiled. *What a jerk!* Mark thought.

The cop stared at him with such contempt Mark took an involuntary step back.

"Victim services are on the second floor, kid," the partner answered. "Might want to watch who you're sassing off to. Someone might take offense and turn you over their knee."

"Second floor? Thank you so much for your kind directions and even kinder advice. I hope you and your partner here have a lovely day." Mark rolled his eyes, then took his time strolling across the seal toward the stairs. Heat from the deputies' stares made the skin on his back crawl.

While not as impressive as the seal on the floor on the old courthouse side, the county seal on the new side carried all the pomp as the old side—gold filigree sealed beneath polished glass against the black marble floor. The large circle contained the *words County of Summit Valley* at the top and Virginia at the bottom. On the left was the word Est., and on the right was the year 1814. An inner circle surrounded a three-quarter picture of the clock tower with the words *Home, Hearth*, and *Pride*.

Taking the stairs two at a time, Mark followed signs to an office labeled Victim Services. The office seemed completely out of place in the austere government cinder block halls. In lieu of harsh fluorescent overhead lighting, the interior office without windows chose warm lamplight, which cast a golden glow that was both comforting and inviting. The floor was covered wall to wall with a thick burgundy rug. Tasteful area rugs ran underneath an imitation cherry wood coffee table and two end tables situated next to comfy-looking recliners. Chairs lined the walls, and not the plastic or vinyl waiting area variety; these were solid wood and padded.

On the coffee table lay a display of current magazines: *Golf Digest, Sports Illustrated, People, House Beautiful, The New Yorker, The Atlantic,* and something called *The New Guard*. Brochures advertising information on state programs lined a rack on the wall. A receptionist sat at a desk, eyeing Mark politely. Her smile was open and friendly, curious but not suspicious.

Mark felt instantly at ease.

"Come in." The receptionist waved a hand. "Early riser, huh?"

"I'm not sure I'm in the right place."

"Well, what are you looking for? Maybe I can help."

"I have this friend…"

"Wait, first things first." She stood up and came around the desk. She was tiny, five feet tall in the modest heels she wore. "Alexandra Grothe. Everyone calls me Lexi." She held out her hand. Mark shook it. She had streaks of pink in her hair.

"Mark Branton."

"Nice to meet you, Mark. Have a seat and tell me about your friend."

Lexi sat in a recliner by the coffee table. Mark selected a seat against the wall a few chairs away from her. She held a clipboard on her lap and scribbled something down. What, Mark had no idea; he'd only told her his name.

"Right, so I have this friend."

"You seem nervous. Don't be. It's just us here. I expected to be alone all day. Surprise! Good surprise." Lexi smiled her strangely disarming smile.

"Well, truth is, I'm not sure what I'm doing here."

"Why don't you tell me about your friend? What happened to…?" Lexi let the question hang.

"Her."

"Her, then. What happened to her?"

"I don't have many friends."

Unfazed by the strange turn in conversation, Lexi answered, "I never had many friends either. The ones I had, I tried to care for. Is this girl special to you? Like a girlfriend?"

"Oh, no. I've never had a girlfriend." Mark stopped, mortified at his confession, then blundered on: "Alicia is friend. Just a friend! I don't have many of those."

"Okay, sorry for assuming. Go on."

Mark tried to dismiss the feeling of being analyzed. Why should he start confessing his life to a stranger? A squirmy itch at the back of his head kept Mark from becoming too comfortable.

"We're guildies."

"Warcraft?"

Mark perked up. "Yeah, you know it?"

Lexi held her pen hand up. "Undead mage."

"Tauren druid!"

"Your friend is in your guild?"

"We raid together. Run dungeons together. Quest together. Or we did until she stopped logging on."

"When did you find out who she was IRL?"

Mark grinned at her use of IRL—in real life. Lexi got it, no doubt about it. "We go to school together, have since we were little."

"So, she stopped logging on?"

"A few weeks ago. Three weeks ago. She had a date."

"Boyfriends can make time online seem less important. It's part of growing up. It doesn't necessarily mean something bad happened to her."

"Normally, I'd agree. But I overheard my boss talking to a guy whose girlfriend works in the trauma ward at the hospital. They were talking about Alicia."

"Your boss was talking to a guy, who dates a girl, who works in the hospital? That's pretty convoluted."

"It was her they were talking about. I know it. They said she'd been raped! Said her father was a janitor. That's Alicia. She hasn't been to school in weeks. I know something's happened."

"Have you notified the police?"

"Like those fat idiots downstairs? What would I notify them of?"

"You could let them know you have concerns. They could do a welfare check."

"No." He shook his head. "I don't want her to get shot. Things never go well for people when the police come to check on their welfare."

"Why would you say that?"

"Because I'm poor. Poor people know the truth. It's all we have."

Lexi's lips pinched together sympathetically. "Back to Alicia. If you aren't interested in telling the police—assuming they aren't already doing their own investigation—what's your plan?"

"I don't know." Mark shrugged. "I'm winging it here. Doing what feels right. I only heard about it this morning at work and figured it had to be her. If Alicia is hurt or needs help, I want to help her."

"Then I have a couple of suggestions. First thing you do is check the hospital. See if she's there. You can call the front desk to ask if she's a patient. I'll even let you use my phone. The second thing you can do is simple. Go see her. Let her know you're around, but don't press her. If she's been hurt, she may not want you around. She may lash out. Be patient with her. If she's been the victim of a sexual assault, give her one of our fliers. We help women in crisis every day."

Lexi handed Mark a brochure. On the cover, a group of women stood painting canvases in the sunshine. Cursive writing at the top read *The COLONY: A Place for Women. A Place for Healing*. Mark flipped the brochure over. On the back, a picture of a smiling Lexi announced her as the director of operations and founder of the Colony.

"You're the boss?" Mark asked. "But you're working on a Saturday."

Lexi laughed, deep and clear. "Why? The boss can't work the weekend? News flash —bosses work harder than most. Besides, it was my turn in the rotation, and I like putting in the hours here. This office is comfy, don't you think?"

"I guess so." Mark shrugged, feeling awkward. "What can I do about the guy who attacked her?"

Lexi shook her head. "Nothing. Revenge isn't a path you want to follow. Right now, you don't even know if you have anything to avenge. Find out if your friend is hurt. If she is, then be her friend. Listen. Don't judge. And don't force her in any particular direction. Give her my information. Sometimes, it's easier for a woman to talk to another woman."

"I just feel like I need to do something more."

"Let's start with a phone call. Here's the number for Summit Valley Community Hospital patient information. Ask if she's a patient. If she is, ask if the family is accepting visitation."

Lexi dialed the number before handing Mark the headset.

Mark left the victim services office feeling better about Alicia's situation. He'd spoken with her on the phone, and she didn't want to see him but said she was grateful for the phone call. Mark thought he might drop off the brochure for the Colony anyway. Maybe leave it with her dad or have a nurse give it to her.

"Fuckin' mistake, that."

Einar stood on the sidewalk, his cowboy hat hiding all but his scraggly jawline.

Mistake? Helping Alicia?

"What are you talking about?" Mark asked. "Where have you been? What's happening to me? Did you see the sparrow? I healed a sparrow!"

Ignoring his questions—Mark almost expected him to at this point—Einar said, "You're not ready for the Colony. Fucking around with Lexi is a bad idea. Almost as bad an idea as pissing life away on birds. We need to talk. It's obvious to me that left on your own, you're going to burn out."

Mark scoffed. "I've only been waiting on an explanation since summer. Take your time. No hurry now."

"Listen"—Einar leaned close, towering over Mark and forcing him to take a step back—"stay away from Lexi and the Colony." He grabbed Mark by the upper arm with an unwavering grip, preventing Mark from moving farther away.

"Fine. Whatever. Let go of my arm."

"She's dangerous. More dangerous than you know. You've yet to fully change, and until you understand—fully understand—you're going to have to trust me."

"How can I trust you?" Mark asked. "You show up randomly, don't explain anything, bark orders, and expect me to fall in line. You did something to me, and now you won't tell me what's happening. I've about accepted that I'll be dealing with these changes on my own anyway."

"You're young and invincible, I get it. Please, Mark, do as I say. Stay away from the Colony."

///

Lucas sat on the couch—a Norfolk U-Sectional, Saltwashed Belgian Linen, retailed shy of $13,000—scowling. He was pissed, and the subtle sophistication of the luxurious furniture and the casual elegance of the room did little to curb his anger. Lucas liked his mother's study. Her perfume, La Vie Est Belle, lingered.

Housekeeping had instructions to refresh the scent in here every two weeks with a bottle his father had bought for the purpose. His mother's actual perfume remained almost empty on her vanity in the same spot she'd left it after its final use. This room—her study, her office, her sanctuary—had become sacred ground after her death. An unspoken shrine to a woman who'd dominated the men in her life just as she'd controlled all others around her.

Lucas missed her. Every day.

Lucas had understood her. She was hard because the people in her life needed her to be. Wayne and later Lucas fell into her orbit, pulled by the unescapable gravity of her. Lucas had been permitted access to her study if he remained silent while she worked. Content to be in her presence, Lucas had often played on the floor, always careful to clean up after himself.

Later, he would sit on this couch, reading, studying, or playing muted video games on a handheld—a living decoration paying silent homage to the woman in the center. Even now, after her death, Lucas wouldn't dare sit at her desk or rifle through her belongings. He had a feeling Wayne didn't either.

Father and son had been thoroughly conditioned not to trespass.

Large picture windows wrapped around her desk, framing it in natural light. Thick crème rugs caressed and cushioned the foot. Oriental area rugs in fuchsia, crème, and turquoise tones complemented the neutral beige of the walls.

Lucas considered killing his father.

Julia would never had allowed for his accident with Alicia. Wayne, on the other hand, beat him for it and said he'd have to give up the Mustang as partial repayment. His Mustang! Did Wayne expect him to walk everywhere now? He was varsity captain this year and was being scouted by major college teams. He could even go pro. He needed a ride.

The beatings he could take. Then humiliation he could not.

Bad enough he'd been knocked on his ass by a freshman in front of everyone, now he was going to have to take the bus? As a senior? Uh, no. Some things were completely unacceptable. He'd give Wayne time to cool off, catch a ride with Ethan for a while, then convince him to give the wheels back. Wayne had only paid out $300K. It wasn't like they were starving.

In fact, Wayne had come back from the hospital smiling. Lucas was grateful there wouldn't be jail time. Not that he'd expected any. He was, after all, rich. But forcing him to give up his car wasn't right. When he pointed out this obvious fact to Wayne, Wayne had backhanded him.

"You have to learn consequences. There are laws for them and laws for us, but there are still laws. Maybe taking away your toys will remind you to take better care. Enjoy it this weekend. Monday, I'm selling it at the dealership."

Lucas had stood there fuming, holding his burning cheek. Breaking eye contact first, Lucas had left for the one place in the house he felt safe: his mother's sanctuary. Sitting on her couch here in her room, smelling the ghost of her perfume, Lucas felt a calm settle over him. Yeah, he'd kill Wayne someday. Patricide, the idea of murdering his father, felt right. Julia approved. He felt it in his heart.

Mark lay in his bed reading over the pamphlet Lexi had given him. Bone shared the bed, large fuzzy head resting on Mark's stomach. Absently scratching Bone's ears, Mark reread the brochure. The Colony was a women's shelter. A safe space for battered and endangered women to rest, recover, seek counseling, and regain a semblance of normalcy. They helped pick up the shattered pieces and reformed them into stronger, more capable people.

Hidden away, protected, and sheltered, the women and children of the Colony took the time necessary to heal. Educational programs for mother and child, job counseling, GED classes, medical help, legal advice, food, shelter, and any other basic needs were met. There was curriculum on dating violence and preventing sexual assault for middle and high school age children as well as programs for older victims.

At-risk mothers and their children, divorcees, addicts, runaways, rich, poor, victims of sexual or domestic violence, and everything in between were welcomed with open arms. The Colony looked to be the exact kind of place to help Alicia.

All he needed to do was figure out how to get her the information without embarrassing her, angering her father, or appearing like a nosy rosy who couldn't mind his own business. Mark didn't ask himself if Alicia wanted his help. The question never occurred to him.

The following morning, Mark woke early to make breakfast. The extra money he'd been earning working at the warehouse meant there was sausage to go with the pancakes. Dad had taught him the secret of a fluffy pancake. He'd even taken his father's recipe a step further, adding fresh fruit or chocolate chips if they had any. As he cooked, his mother came into the kitchen for her morning coffee.

"Morning, baby. What's for breakfast?" she asked.

"Pancakes and sausage. I figured you might not want the cakes, so I kept an egg back. I saw a block of cheese in the fridge. We can shred into some scrambled eggs if you want."

"Mmm. Can't I have both?"

"Sure. Get some coffee. Have a seat. I'll have breakfast ready in a flash."

Mark smiled while grating cheddar. He and his mother saw each other so little. She worked, and he went to school and had a part-time job. This meant they relished any time together.

She amazed him. She worked so hard to keep the two of them fed, clothed, and sheltered.

Mark loved her.

After mixing a dollop of sour cream into the eggs—Dad insisted this was the secret ingredient for the greatest scrambled eggs on the planet—Mark poured the egg mixture into the hot pan he'd cooked the sausage in. Using the little bit of grease for additional flavor, Mark mixed in the cheese, careful to keep agitating to prevent scalding. A quick few minutes later, breakfast was served: scrambled eggs, sausage, pancakes, a refill on coffee for Mom, and a glass of orange juice for him. They ate in silence, enjoying the meal as well as the company. Neither felt the need to yammer on.

"What do you have planned for today? Working?" Mom asked, breaking the quiet clink of fork to plate.

"Not today. Warehouse is closed on Sunday. What about you? Church?"

"I thought I might see what I can get into. Becky's been to a new winery."

"Sounds like a wild time, Mom."

"I'm a wild woman who can't be stopped." She took the last bite of her eggs. "Thank you for breakfast. It was delicious."

"It was, wasn't it?"

"Since you cooked, I'll do the dishes."

"I tried to clean up as I went along. Somebody taught me that if I do, the mess at the end isn't so bad."

"Who taught you that?"

"Some chick named Sabrina." Mark grinned at his mother.

Sabrina raised an eyebrow. "She sounds like a smart lady."

"She's okay, I guess. Better than a stick in the eye."

She threw a dishrag at him.

Mark checked his watch. 7:37. He stretched and made the spontaneous decision to check out the Colony. Doing something, anything, to help Alicia had remained on the forefront of his mind since hearing about her attack. While he hadn't been to visit her, he had every intention of doing so. Telling her about the Colony in person felt right.

Having gone over the route several times last night and a few more times before breakfast, Mark felt confident he'd find the way.

I can do this faster without shoes.

Mark leaned back inside and grabbed his backpack. He removed his shoes and socks, then placed them in the bag atop a pack of teaberry gum and a few sticks of teriyaki beef jerky. Mark always felt hungry, and the protein helped curb the worst hunger pangs. The Colony was located out where Randolph Avenue became state Route 738, which meant Mark had a long trip ahead of him. Having a few snacks helped. After slipping the pack on, tightening the shoulder straps, and fastening the wimp strap around his waist, Mark headed out.

Mark planned to keep track of landmarks along the way to judge how far he still needed to go. He'd pass the funeral home; United Holiness across from United Methodist; Summit Valley Cemetery; the old WBAD radio station, which was rumored to be haunted, Blenkins Vineyard; Kents Chapel; Summit Valley Apostolic Church; ABC Small Engine Repair, who worked on Mark's lawn mower when needed; Trinity Baptist; and finally Colony Branch Road. All told, he'd have a thirty-mile round trip.

The thought didn't intimidate him in the least.

Streets in Summit Valley were silent that early Sunday morning, except for the rhythmic slap of Mark's feet against the asphalt. It was too early for church traffic. Mark skirted the western edge of downtown Summit Valley, the skyline dominated by the old courthouse clock tower. A dog barked as he passed the funeral home, and the barking followed him as far as the fence allowed. Mark ran on.

The morning, overcast and cool, promised no warmth for the day but filled Mark's lungs with crisp air. Moving faster than an Olympic sprinter, Mark knew he had more but didn't want to open up until downtown faded behind him. He waited for the houses to thin and sit farther back from the road before pouring it on.

United Holiness passed in a blur on his left, the parking lot empty save for the preacher's Cadillac. Mark pumped his arms, leaning into the run. Air whistled past his ears, pinning his hair back from his forehead. A popping sound momentarily broke his concentration until he realized it was his just shirt popping in the breeze.

His feet didn't seem to touch the street. The sidewalk ended after the cemetery, forcing Mark to run on the edge of the road. As he rounded a corner, trees flashing by in a blur, an old Ford truck turned too sharply, edging into Mark's lane. Instinct moved Mark out of the way and closer to the edge before he entered the corner. The truck driver blared his horn, overcorrecting, then jerking back onto the correct side of the road.

Later, the driver would wonder if the kid-shaped blur was even real. Maybe it was a haunt from the old radio station.

WBAD disappeared behind him. When Mark crested a hill, the countryside lay before him, free of the trees crowding the road. Mark didn't stop to admire the scenery. Part of his mind registered the pastures, brown now this close to winter; the clumps of cows dotting distant hillsides, clustered together for warmth; and the skeletal trees, bare limbs scraping the overcast sky, but most of his focus remained on the road beneath his feet.

Hairpin turns proved difficult to navigate. His speed pulled him toward the center of the road, dangerous should there be another oncoming truck. Forced to slow as the road dipped and turned more frequently, Mark's frustration rose. His heart beat steadily in his chest, and his breath came deep and regular. A fine perspiration dotted along his forehead and quickly cooled.

As he climbed out of the holler, the road straightened out somewhat. Mark was filled with the joy of speed as he ran faster than before, his previous impatience fueling recklessness. ABC passed in a blip, barely registered. Mark recognized Colony Road as he passed. He tried to stop, slid in the gravel, and fell.

Rolling end over end, Mark slid thirty feet before a tree arrested his momentum. The air rushed out of his lungs in a great "Ugh, uhhh!"

Mark lay on his side, stomach against a large white oak, waves of pain cascading through him. His pant legs had ripped open at the knees, the fabric torn and his skin flayed by gravel when Mark tried to catch himself. Knees and palms leaked pin drops of blood. The worst pain came from his chest where he'd slammed into the tree.

Are my ribs broken? Mark wondered.

Rolling over and away from the oak, Mark got to his hands and knees. Something popped in his left side. Immediately, the pain receded, replaced by a deep itch. Mark stood up. Sometime during the run, his feet had transformed again—thicker and covered in a black scale that reabsorbed into his skin while he watched his feet shrink back to their normal size tens. His legs felt depleted, weak, the muscles shaking in exhaustion. Large claws receded into his toes, as did the thick hook at his heel.

That's how I held the road at speed. I didn't even feel it happen.

Looking at the road, Mark could clearly see the path he'd run, ending in two deep trenches gouged into the earth. A quick diagnostic on himself revealed that, other than his shaky legs, he felt great. The droplets of blood on his hands and knees belied any injury underneath. The skin was dirty but smooth, unblemished. Slapping dust from his shirt and pants, Mark fingered the holes at his knees.

Great. Something else I need to fix before Mom sees.

Mark walked back toward Colony Road, wiping more dust and debris off his sleeves and hips. His backpack had remained securely fastened—no damage there. Checking his watch, Mark stopped. 7:52. He must have broken the watch in his fall, although the crystal face wasn't cracked and the second hand ticked along like always. Unless he misremembered his start time, his run had taken only fifteen minutes. He'd run a mile a minute.

Sixty miles an hour.

I'm trying out for track.

Early morning overcast skies showed no signs of relenting their hold on the heavens. Thick cool air promised cold rain later in the afternoon, and Mark hoped his business concluded before the clouds cut loose. A light breeze tousled his sweaty hair, and he reflexively smoothed it out with his hand.

Colony Road led off into pastureland, through rolling hills bordered on either side with well-maintained three-slat split fencing. Fresh paint, applied recently, shone bright in contrast with the morning gloom. Without the slap of his feet on the asphalt and the rush of wind past his ears, the countryside was silent.

A hundred meters farther, the road switched from asphalt to gravel. Mark shifted right, choosing to walk in the rut worn by passing traffic. Mark followed the painted fence line into Colony property. Another half mile through woods saw Mark to a small guard shack. A barrier gate connected to the fence blocked further progression.

Apparently, a security guard was supposed to monitor visitors to the grounds, but the booth stood empty, door ajar. A Town & Country magazine lay open on the small desk, pages rustling in the breeze. There wasn't any traffic this close to the Colony, but still, for a place that advertised security and protection, Mark found the lack of a guard troubling.

"I'm going to ask you again to leave this place be."

Mark turned around. Einar sat on the fence.

"You don't know what you're getting into here. I won't follow you inside."

Mark considered Einar's warning. "Well, who asked you to?"

"Are you sure?"

"Am I sure? About helping Alicia? Yes, I'm sure."

"Did she ask you for help?"

"She's my friend. I don't have many of those."

Einar shook his head. "Since you won't be talked out of this foolishness, go ahead. I'll see you tonight if you don't end up like him." He jerked his chin up the gravel drive.

The security guard walked up to the booth, a can of paint in his hand, murmuring to himself. "She said paint the fence. The whole fence. Gotta paint the fence. The whole fence."

White paint speckled the guard's uniform. Blotches of paint splatter stained nearly every inch of him, from his shaggy dark hair to his scuffed military style boots, one of which was untied, laces dragging. A name tag identified him as William.

Einar was gone. Again.

"Uh, hey," Mark said, turning to the guard. "I was wondering if I could talk to Lexi."

"She said paint the fence. The whole fence." William didn't seem to be aware of Mark.

"Right…"

"Gotta paint the whole fence."

"You might want to put that job off for a while. I think it's going to rain."

"She said paint the fence. The whole fence."

"Okay, you paint the whole fence, and I'm going to see Lexi."

"Gotta paint the whole fence."

William popped the can open with a large knife he'd produced from within his coat. Mark headed in the direction William had come from, and William resumed mumbling to himself.

Guy must be some type of affirmative action hire, Mark thought. Functions high enough to do small tasks, like sit in the booth all day or paint the fence, but not suited for much more.

From the road, Mark noticed easels set atop a hillside, though they were empty now. Either too early for painting or threatening weather kept the artists away. The view offered a panoramic view of the Blue Ridge Mountains. Past the artist's hill, a wide well-manicured lawn surrounded several dome-shaped buildings. Smaller pods encircled a large central dome.

People, the majority female, busied themselves around the structure. A few men on ladders worked on a new dome. A group of women held a class on the lawn. Karate? Tai Chi? Yoga? The instructor, dressed in a white T-shirt, jeans, and white low-top shoes, led a group of thirty or so through a variety of poses. While everyone was dressed similarly, not everyone wore white. The men working wore the same uniform as William: coat, pants, blue button-down shirt, and name tag.

Mark headed toward the group of women working out on the lawn. As he got closer, he noticed Lexi led the group. Even with the chaotic nature of activity around the buildings, everyone seemed to move with a purpose. Though when Mark neared Lexi, that movement ceased, and everyone turned to face him as if on cue.

"Hello again, Mark. Care to join us?" Turning her back to the group, Lexi favored Mark with a smile.

People began moving, busy again, the interruption forgotten. An unidentified fear squirmed in Mark's stomach at the invitation.

"Uh, no. Actually, I wanted to continue our conversation about my friend."

"Alicia?"

"Yes."

"No." Lexi held up a finger as she called back over her shoulder: "Alicia!"

Mark's jaw dropped when Alicia separated herself from the group and moved to stand beside Lexi. Faded bruises marred her cheeks, and her left arm lay across her chest in a sling. She was dressed in the same uniform as the other women.

"Hi." Alicia gave Mark a small wave with her good hand.

Lexi laughed. "Don't look so shocked, Mark. After we spoke, I went to the hospital, and Alicia and I hit it off. I convinced her father a short stay here would be good for her. He agreed. She agreed. Here we are." She smiled first at Mark, then Alicia. "Alicia, why don't you rejoin the class, and I'll walk your friend out." Lexi motioned to a small brunette standing just behind Alicia. "Take over, Claire. Please and thank you."

Claire nodded, assuming position.

Lexi took Mark's arm and led him away from Alicia, back toward the road. "I trust seeing your friend here has answered whatever questions you had for me?"

Mark felt confused. A thousand questions buzzed around his head, all of which avoided his tongue. "I wanted—now I'm not sure what I wanted. I guess I wanted Alicia to get help."

"She has it. She's safer here than anywhere on earth. We'll take good care of her."

"What about the guy who hurt her?"

"Lucas?"

"Yeah."

"What about him?" Lexi asked.

"Is Alicia going to send him to jail?"

"I'm sure she wouldn't want me discussing her business."

"He can't be allowed to get away with this!" Mark was horrified just by the thought.

"Karma comes around. Mr. Foster arranged for Mr. Gahan to pay for her stay, and I assure you, we aren't cheap."

"That's it? Karma? You get paid?" Mark refused to believe his ears.

"What would you like to be done? Alicia is the one hurt. She's the victim here. Forget about Lucas, and focus on her."

"It's not right. He needs to pay."

"And you're what? Her avenging angel? Leave this alone, Mark. Your heart is in the right place, but this isn't your business anymore. It never was. You need to go home and think about your motivations. Why are you here? Why do you want revenge? For Alicia? Or is it for you?"

Mark didn't have a reply. His head was swimming. He'd come here thinking he'd find Alicia some type of help, and help had already arrived.

Lexi softened her tone. "Take solace in the fact that you got the ball rolling. Coming to see me was a good thing. Alicia can heal here with no burden on her family. When she's ready to rejoin the world, she will. Until then, relax." Lexi punched him playfully in the shoulder. "I got this."

Back at the security booth, William continued painting, oblivious to their arrival.

"What's his deal?" Mark asked.

"William? He used to date Claire. The lady who took over my class back there? Anyway, he was abusive."

"You gave him a job?"

"He's harmless now."

"I thought you said he was an abuser."

"He's changed. Seen the error of his ways." Lexi faced him, changing the subject. "Stay away. Give her time."

Mark nodded, unsure of what else to do. Lexi nodded, turned, and headed back down the road. Feeling dismissed, Mark watched Lexi head back toward her strange group—a group Mark clearly wasn't part of. As he walked to the property edge, Mark understood this was a goodbye. Alicia had moved out of his life. No more raids. No more guilds.

Attempting to shake off his sudden case of blues, he took his shoes off and stuffed them into his backpack. *Maybe I can beat my time.* Mark began to sprint. Fast as he was he couldn't outrun his sense of loss.

Back at home, twelve minutes later, Mark sat on his bed picking small rocks from between the scales on the bottom of his feet and tossing them into the trash. The rocks hit with a small *swish-ping!* A swish when the gravel hit the trash bag, a ping when the rock fell to the metal bottom of the can.

If he concentrated, he could extend and retract the claws. What was happening to him?

Swish-ping!

What was he becoming?

Swish-ping!

Bone lay across the room, curled in front of his closet, watching the process with canine intensity. Whatever was happening, it didn't have Bone alarmed. He'd greeted Mark at the door like he always did, tail wagging, bashing off the walls while spinning in circles.

Mom had left for church while he was out—something she did on occasion. Church wasn't a steady thing for either of them, though Mark considered himself a spiritual person. They had their faith, and that was enough. Neither felt the need to—pardon the pun—religiously attend every Sunday.

Wonder what Pastor would think of this? Mark thought, extending the thick heel claws. *Probably think I was possessed and throw me out of the building.*

If Mom went to church, she was feeling lonely. Mark expected she'd spend much of the day out and come home late that night, depending on her work schedule. She worked too much and didn't have a boyfriend. Mark didn't begrudge her some adult company. She'd assist with whatever volunteer program was happening after worship. Then she'd have dinner with Becky, who was the closest thing she had to a friend and also a widow. The two of them would drink wine, play cards, or both until she felt like coming home.

On the rare Sundays she went out, Mark didn't expect to see her until Monday after school. Mark loved her, and he knew she loved him. Sometimes, she needed to be a grown-up—not easy with a kid at home. Now that he was a teenager and had a job, she trusted him to take care of himself.

Mark's thoughts drifted back to the Colony. Specifically, the way everyone had stopped moving and stared upon his arrival. There was no denying the sudden threat in the air. Creepy. And the way the security guard, William, had been so single-minded...

He's changed, Lexi had said.

The silver claws withdrew completely.

Seen the error.

Then they popped out, reflecting sunlight around the room.

Changed.

In.

Blank faces staring in quiet menace.

Out.

Seen the error.

Swish-ping!

If I'd been aggressive, those people would have torn me apart.

In.

Seen the error.

Out.

"You're not wrong."

A low growl from Bone confirmed Mark was no longer alone. Two sparrows landed on the windowsill and pecked at the glass. Einar leaned against the doorway. All three appeared to be waiting for an invitation to come in.

"How do you do that?" Mark asked.

"Do what?"

"Appear and disappear at will."

"I don't. You're getting better at controlling your feet."

"I know. Don't change the subject."

"I didn't," Einar said.

Mark shook his head. "Why do I even talk to you?"

"I'm charming."

Mark met this comment with a flat gaze. "Is that what you'd call it?"

Einar nodded. "I would. Now, before we get down to business—and we have some serious business to get to—we eat, yes? I never get into transformation instruction on an empty stomach."

"I ate breakfast already."

"Well, I have not. Besides, you had a little run, which I'm sure worked up a bit of an appetite. You're a growing boy, after all. Growing boys can always eat."

Mark rolled his eyes. Einar made it hard to remain disagreeable, but the teenager in Mark felt up to the challenge. "I guess so. If that's what it takes to move forward."

"Excellent." Einar rubbed his hands together, creating a swishing sound that left Mark with the uncomfortable image of a hissing snake. "To the kitchen, then. I'll cook."

Einar proved to be a remarkable chef. From the refrigerator came sliced ham, shaved turkey, mustard, Swiss cheese, eggs, milk, butter, and raspberry jam. Out of the pantry, Einar fetched bread—the thick French kind his mother used for garlic bread on spaghetti nights—honey, and powdered sugar.

"What are you doing?" Mark snurled his nose.

"Patience, dear boy. Allow me to concentrate!"

Mark slouched at the table, watching Einar with interest.

"Where are your knives? Oh! Never mind. I found them."

Einar sliced four pieces of bread, hesitated, then sliced two more. In a small bowl, he mixed a blob of mustard with honey, then set it aside. In another bowl, he mixed two eggs, milk, nutmeg, and cinnamon, along with a bit of vanilla extract. After stacking the meats and cheese on the bread following a generous dollop of honey mustard, Einar carefully dipped the sandwiches in the egg batter. He set the dripping sandwiches in a pan of melted butter and fried each side to a golden brown. Then he sliced the sandwiches in half, dusted them with powdered sugar, and served Mark's with a side of raspberry jam.

Bone lay under the table, casting wary glances between Mark and Einar.

"What's this?" Mark asked.

"That, dear boy, is a Monte Cristo. Kind of a souped-up grilled cheese I find makes an excellent brunch sandwich. It's just the right combination of sweet and savory."

"I think it's closer to a stuffed French toast. Whatever, it's delicious."

"Whichever works for you," Einar said.

Despite having eaten with Mom, Mark devoured his sandwich. Einar set another in front of him, which

Mark transformed into crumbs and jam smears while tearing small bites off for Bone.

As they ate, they spoke of nothing consequential. Mark tried learning more about Einar; however, Einar danced around every question without answering. Mark left the table feeling like he knew less about Einar than when they sat down.

"It's time we got down to business," Einar eventually said. "Before we do, however, I need you to take care of a small matter."

"And that would be what?" Mark asked, instantly wary.

"Put the dog up. Outside. Wherever. I need to concentrate, and I can't hold the dog back and focus my attention on you at once."

"What are you talking about? Put Bone outside?"

"Which question would you like an answer to?" Einar asked.

"Huh?"

"Ask one question at a time, get one answer at a time. Avoids confusion."

Mark thought for a moment. "Why do I need to put Bone outside?"

"I answered this one already. Because I need to concentrate."

"Bone isn't going to bother you. He hung out by my feet during lunch without bothering anybody."

"Oh, I'm sorry." Einar cocked his head in irritation. "I've never done this before and don't know what I'm talking about."

"Sorry, sorry." Mark held up his hand. "Bone is a good dog. That's all I'm saying."

"I'm sure he is." Einar relaxed his tone somewhat, although a deep wrinkle remained between his brows. "But this isn't like the woods. I need total concentration to keep you from killing both of us. I can't do that while holding your panicked dog at bay."

"What do you mean kill us both?"

"Put the dog outside. Now." Einar's tone hardened again.

"Fine!" Mark slapped his thigh. "Come on, Bone."

Mark held the side door open, and Bone trotted into the yard, headed for the tree line. He turned around to see if Mark had followed him, but he'd already closed the door. So Bone lay down on the porch, waiting on the door to open, waiting for his boy.

Deciding the living room did not provide enough privacy, the pair ended up in Mark's room.

"No, this won't do." Einar shook his head. "Is there no privacy in this house?"

"No one is coming into my room. Mom won't be home for hours yet."

"No, this isn't going to work. Let the dog back in."

"What? You threw a fit for me to put him out!"

"I remember. I was there."

"What happened to 'I've done this before'?" Mark asked, doing a fair impression of Einar.

"Sounds nothing like me. And that was before I realized the deplorable lack of privacy in here."

"Okay, then. So now what?"

"I propose a race."

"A race," Mark said.

"Yes. Let your doggo in, and we'll race to Coopers Cave."

"I'm confused."

"Privacy, dear boy. There, we can remain undisturbed."

"So why race?"

"Keeps things interesting," Einar said. "And I'll offer you a wager. If you beat me, I'll answer all the questions I see swimming around in your head."

"And if I lose?"

"*When* you lose, you'll keep those questions to yourself and do what I tell you to do."

"Fine." Mark grinned at Einar. "Let's do it."

"Pack a change of clothes."

"Why? I can't stay out on a school night. Mom'll be mad."

"Always with the questions. Put a change of clothes in your backpack!" Einar threw his hands up and stomped out of Mark's room.

Mark grinned again and threw a quick change, including his shoes, into his backpack. Tightening the belt around his waist, he went downstairs to find Einar back at the kitchen table.

"Ready?" Einar asked.

"Ready."

"Good boy. Let's go."

Mark opened the front door, and Bone bumped his leg as he ran back inside. "Let me lock the door and—hey!"

Einar sprinted past Bone, who slid and fell on the tile in his attempt to get turned around, shot past Mark, and covered fifty yards of open yard before Mark could finish a sentence. He vanished among the shadows of the tree line at the edge of the property

Einar was fast.

Mark slammed the door, jammed the key in the lock, and twisted the key too far in his rush. After losing precious seconds wrestling with the key, Mark neither heard nor saw any sign of Einar.

"Dirty cheater!" Mark yelled as he started to run.

Adrenaline flooded his system. Mark's leg muscles thickened. Silver claws punched out of his toes, and the large heel claws broke free with a small splash of blood. Heightened senses told him Bone was inside barking. Einar was somewhere ahead of him, crashing through the trees and making so much noise Mark wondered how he hadn't heard him before.

Mark dashed into the woods, covering the open ground in seconds.

Blackberry bushes, winter dry, stretched their thorny branches across the trail. Mark plowed them underfoot without a thought, protected by his thick scales. With his eyes adjusted to the shadows, Mark followed in Einar's footsteps. He'd left a clear path of destruction. Young trees were snapped off and stomped into the mud. The ground, gouged and torn, pointed the way.

Einar had apparently run through or over anything in his way. As Mark sprinted faster and faster still, he dodged the larger trees collapsing across the trail, their mangled bases unable to support their ancient weight with half or more of their diameter blown to splinters by Einar. It was like a real-life cartoon. Mark shuddered as he considered one of the massive behemoths falling on him.

Leaping, dodging, and running a twisting path to avoid Einar's mess, Mark sensed him pulling farther ahead. Moving away from Einar's trail, Mark straightened his course. He caught a grapevine and swung across Peak Creek, launching himself thirty feet past the opposite bank, never breaking stride. Mark began the long ascent up the mountain to Coopers Cave.

Einar, somewhere ahead but closer now, continued crashing through the woods. To Mark, he sounded like the end of the world: pounding feet, exploding trees, snapping branches, and even the cracking of stone. Whatever Einar was, he was powerful. Refusing to be intimidated, Mark ran on. He was faster, and he knew it. Heart pumping, lungs heaving, Mark opened himself up like never before. In the final uphill stretch, Mark caught sight of Einar, a few hundred yards ahead of him. Slowing.

As he leaned into the hill and concentrated only on more speed, the wind roared in Mark's ears. The scenery flashed by, a blur in his periphery, unimportant. Crashing trees cried their final lament to no one, booming to the earth behind him. Always behind him. Impact tremors vibrated through the soles of his feet. Einar's heavy tread, one step for every three of Marks. Gaining, gaining.

Got him!

Mark whooped in triumph. Einar stopped running, standing perfectly still next to Mark's old campfire. At his current speed, Mark couldn't stop. He overshot the campground, ripping into the bush on the far side.

Mark tried to stop by digging his claws in. His feet dug into the stone until the stone ran out.

He went airborne, arms pinwheeling, having run off the cliff overlooking the Deer Hole. A little faster and I might have cleared it, Mark thought before plummeting into the water. A rain of sticks, dirt, stone, leaves and debris followed him.

Mark plodded his soggy way back up to the campsite, relieved to see Einar had started a fire in the pit. His back was to Mark as he strung a line up near the fire for Mark to hang his wet clothes on. Everything in his backpack was wet too. Mark hadn't put anything in Ziplocs in his rush to leave. He dropped his pack by the fire and sat down, grateful for the warmth.

"Did you enjoy your swim? It's a bit chilly for my taste, but some people swear a cold swim keeps you healthy."

Mark glared at Einar.

"Why the mad face? I didn't run you off the cliff."

Instead of answering, Mark scooted closer to the fire.

"Here." Einar handed Mark a blanket—the one off his own bed. "Hang your wet clothes and bundle up."

"Where did this come from?" Mark asked.

"From your room, off your very own bed. Don't you recognize it?"

"Yeah, but how did you get it?"

"Enough questions. You lost. Do as you're told."

Mark sighed, stomping off to the cave to strip out of his wet clothes. A few moments later, he emerged from the cave wrapped in his blanket, his clothes in a wet ball in his hand. Einar had removed the wet clothing from Mark's bag and hung them to dry. He'd placed his shoes near the fire.

"Excellent. Hang those too." Einar motioned toward the dripping bundle in Mark's hand. "They'll smell like smoke, but they'll be nice and dry for your return home."

"Speaking of, we can't stay out here all night. Mom is going to worry."

"I'll take full responsibility."

Mark rolled his eyes. "I'm sure that will make her feel better."

"I think so. Now, let's begin."

Pain. Never-ending pain unlike anything he'd felt before ravaged through his body. An involuntary scream ripped from his throat. Muscle fibers burned as they tore, rebuilt, and tore again, forming thick new ropy layers. All of his skin itched as scales forced their way out, covering his body in the beginnings of a thick black armor.

"Yes, boy, let it happen. Keep your eyes on me." Einar knelt by his side, encouraging the madness, using his own will to push Mark through the pain barrier.

"It *hurts!*" Mark screamed as his facial bones broke, reforming into the reptile. His body hair slid off, neatly severed by his scaly plating. Some clung in random patches to his changing skull. Two large blisters on his back swelled and filled with blood before bursting in a crimson splash, freeing the bat-like wings within.

Rolling to his stomach, Mark tried to crawl away from the pain consuming him. Surely this would kill him. He screamed again. Large silver claws burst from his fingertips as his hands blackened, then lengthened and thickened, gaining an extra knuckle per finger. Mark caught a flash of his burning face in the distorted curvature of his claws. His eyes burned red, and a double row of sharpened teeth pushed his old ones out.

Some he swallowed; most fell to earth in a foaming bloody drool.

"Push, boy! Push! You're almost there." Einar's voice had changed, sounding now like boulders grinding, crushing upheaving earth, deep and terrifying.

Mark continued crawling to he didn't know where. Hands and feet dug deep rifts in the stone, pulling him away, away from the awful burning pain wracking his body. His newly formed wings stretched and flapped, vaulting him into the air.

A hand—Einar's—grabbed his ankle and pulled him back toward the fire. He slammed him into the ground and held fast. "No, young lord. You cannot fly away."

Tucking his wings, the reptile rolled, slashing with his foreclaws. Einar caught the blow before the claws raked across his face. Partially changed as well, Einar's lower jaw now resembled a bulldog's—if that bulldog were carved from granite. His arms had thickened, apelike, and held the powerful new reptile with ease. Einar's ears now stood out large and prominent, coming to sharp points near the top of his hairless head.

His gargoyle wings, folded on his back, framed his heavy visage.

Einar crouched over the squirming reptile, who snapped, hissing in fury.

Listen to me, Lord Reptile, hear my voice. Be still.

Release me!

I cannot. You will hurt yourself trying to hurt me. Be calm, Lord Reptile. Be still.

How is it that we speak? Your mouth does not move, rock face.

I speak to your mind, as you speak to mine.

Release me.

Very well. Do not try to harm me.

Einar released him, then took two knuckle-walking steps backward. The reptile, free from constraint, spun and leapt to the top of the leaning stones above the entrance to Coopers Cave. Crouched on rear legs, the reptile stretched, wings extended, neck arched, head to the sky, roaring his triumph.

Einar crouched perfectly still, watching.

Before him was something that hadn't walked the earth in over a thousand years. Einar felt an awe he rarely experienced. The reptile, black scales shimmering like liquid shadow contrasted against the silver of its belly and claws. Small silver barbs tipped the finger bones of the thumb and end of each finger, all wrapped in the silken membrane of wing. A sleek ridge of spines ran from the head and tapered off along the muscled tail. Reflected in the dying firelight, the reptile's eyes glowed red, fierce, and intelligent. Its black pupils split rose gold irises down the middle and focused on him.

You are beautiful, Lord Reptile.

You flatter.

I speak plainly. Never have I heard the stones sing your song. I am humbled to witness your becoming.

Enough. I hunger.

Can you fly? Einar asked.

I can.

Let us hunt.

Evening came clear and cold. The storm that had threatened all day blew out of the area without delivering, and the temperature dropped to near freezing. Stars blinked into existence, bright and distant, offering light but no warmth. The moon hung low on the horizon, yellow and dirty, too tired to rise above distant ridgelines.

Two shadows glided through the evening sky above unpopulated wood. Invisible against the darkening sky, the pair circled a sounder of feral pigs. Three large sows, two boars, six juveniles, and a dozen piglets rooted the forest floor, unaware of the danger circling above.

The pair descended to feed.

///

Stars circled the sky in their endless course, and moonlight reflected off the tops of clouds, sweet and silver. Sharp cold winter wind slid unnoticed off insulated scales as black as the void above. Riding the storm currents, the reptile circled high above Summit Valley. All but invisible from the ground, he luxuriated in the sensation of flight.

Alone now—he'd left Einar to continue to slaughter and feed—he completed slow circles above the town, moving inexorably away from the lights of civilization and toward home. The boy worried about his mother.

Easy, little brother. Tonight, we fly! Eventually, the reptile would take him back home. But for now, it was good to be cradled by the night.

Book II
The Colony

For the next three years, Mark learned to hear the Song of the Stones. Einar taught him what he knew of the old ways and about lycanthropes, the wolf, bear, wasp, gargoyle, and reptile. Mark picked up another warehouse job in addition to National Linen. Renfro Socks, managed by a friend of Millie's, had hired him to do similar work.

Things eased up financially with Sabrina's two jobs and Mark's under-the-table warehouse work. Between school and work, the pair didn't spend much time together. During the summer between his junior and senior years, Summit Valley made national news when a fire consumed most of the county. Mark and Sabrina had been celebrating a rare mother-son night off together by taking Bone to Carters Park in Wythe County. They'd been eating Subway for dinner while allowing Bone off leash to chase ducks when they noticed the glow. The mountains shone like sunset as an uncontrollable fire swept through Summit Valley and the surrounding countryside. State police blocked all roads into town until the fire burned itself out.

Sabrina, Mark, and Dogbone arrived home to find they had no home.

National attention put pressure on politicians, who in turn put pressure on insurance companies to expedite the rebuilding process. Help poured in from all over the country to aid those affected. By October, Mark and Sabrina had moved from the Comfort Inn in Nilbud to their rebuilt home on Caseknife.

It wasn't built by his grandfather's hands, but it felt good nonetheless.

People moved back. Businesses lost were rebuilt. A small economic boom occurred in the county. Dead trees needed to be cleared. Burned-down abandoned homes needed to be bulldozed. The community rallied, and the disaster brought out the best in people. They shoveled, repaved, replanted, rebuilt, and resumed their daily activities. Schools opened to the relief of both parents and their children. People still needed to eat and a place to lay their head at night, and so life returned to normal, more or less.

At the time, Mark had thought their long night had finally ended. He couldn't have been more wrong.

A hard slap between the shoulder blades brought Lucas out of a sound sleep. "Wake up, stupid. You don't get to lie around all day on my dime."

"Ow. What'd you hit me for?"

"Since you're too dumb to stay in school, you're going to work. Get your ass to the dealership," Wayne said.

"I'm not too dumb," Lucas muttered under his breath.

"Well, you're too stupid to control your dick. I'm glad your mother isn't around to see you. Pathetic." Wayne glared at his idiot progeny. Why did the Lord test him with such an incompetent hard-on of a son? Julia would have died of embarrassment if God hadn't already called her home. He'd given Lucas too much, been too indulgent, covered up for him. And now the boy expected to get away with everything.

Time for him to start pulling his weight.

Wayne had kept him out of jail again and again. He'd suppressed charges, intimidated or bought off families, bribed, cajoled—in short, he'd done everything a good father does to protect his child. The boy wanted for nothing. Wayne had hired athletic trainers, tutors, and met every need or want the boy had. And how was he repaid? With disappointment. With heartbreak.

This last episode had been the turning point for Wayne. He gave up. Lucas had had a full athletic scholarship to the University of Virginia. A freshmen quarterback destined for greatness. But Lucas couldn't keep his urges in check. Plenty of girls threw themselves at him, rising star that he was, but Lucas wanted to take.

Being caught in the act of attacking a drunken girl behind a dumpster proved too much for the school to overlook. Lucas was arrested, and Wayne bailed him out. Judge Tower, being a family friend, sentenced Lucas to probation. The school kicked Lucas out despite generous contributions from Wayne. They revoked his scholarship. No one else wanted him. Lucas's face was blasted all over the news. Social media erupted over the outrageously light sentence. Judge Tower resigned.

The whole sorry business was a goddamn grade A cock-up.

Lucas came back home a year after leaving. Wayne let him lie low for a year. Hanging around the house, he couldn't get in trouble; Wayne made sure of that. After another year, news moved on, and Wayne put Lucas to work at the dealership. Lucas didn't want to, but Wayne cared fuck all for what Lucas wanted now.

Not when he'd pissed away everything.

Lucas got out of bed, one hand rubbing at the sore spot on his back where Wayne had hit him, which was already turning bright red with a deeper purple center. Wayne looked at his son—twenty years old, life ruined, hair in corkscrews, sleep still in his eyes, full lips turned down in a scowl. Julia had loved her sleepy boy. Wayne hit him again, in the face this time.

"Dad! What was that for? I'm up!"

"That was for fucking up your life. Now shut your mouth before you get another. Looking at you makes me sick."

Wayne turned and left so Lucas could prepare for the day.

///

Lucas came downstairs, showered and dressed.

"Why are you wearing a suit?" Wayne asked.

"So, I can sell cars," Lucas answered.

"Men sell cars."

"Yeah, hence the suit."

"No." Wayne shook his head. "Men control themselves. You'll be washing cars. You don't get to deal with the public. A woman might come in, and I don't want you raping her before we can make the sale."

"Dad!"

"What? You wash cars and stay the fuck away from my customers. I won't have you abusing the people who pay our rent. I'm all done bailing your dumb ass out of trouble because you can't handle your women."

Lucas hung his head, face flushed. "Fine. I'll go change."

"No time, princess. You're washing cars in a suit."

Lucas slid past his father. "Whatever."

"Baby, let's go buy you a car!"

Ciara smiled at her father. "Really?"

"I told you when we moved that I'd get you a new car for your senior year. I can't believe my baby is a senior in high school. When did that happen?"

"Daddy, stop." Ciara's deep green eyes sparkled at her father, loving him and loving their game. She'd been furious when he told her they were moving to Summit Valley, Virginia—wherever the hell that was—for her senior year, which meant she'd graduate high school with a bunch of strangers. All her friends were in Summerville.

Daddy said the car was to her get back and forth to school. Ciara knew a bribe when she saw one.

Granted, she knew he didn't have much choice in the move. Volvo needed him to streamline the plant in

Summit Valley like he'd done in South Carolina. He was brilliant, and she loved him, and she'd fully take advantage of a car. She'd be going to college next year, and a vehicle was a must. She loved her parents, but like any seventeen-year-old girl, she couldn't wait to get out on her own.

"My Lord, Trent, you spoil her," Ciara's mother said.

"I love her. Besides, she's old enough. She can help us with groceries, take herself to school—"

"Date," Ciara added, winking at her mother.

"We'll get something that ejects boy butts from the car. No dating until you're thirty-five. You know this."

"Dad!"

Lucas hung his coat in his locker and rolled up his sleeves.

"My, if you aren't the prettiest little car washer I've ever seen."

"Eat my ass, Brandon." Lucas smiled and gave him the finger.

"Seriously, why the suit?"

"Thought I'd be on the sales floor today."

"You're never going to be on the sales floor. Daddy's mad at you." Brandon laughed. "I think I might have a spare coverall if you want."

"Nah. That'd just get you in trouble too. If the suit gets ruined, fuck it, oh well. Wayne paid for it."

Brandon shrugged his thick shoulders. "Whatever you want, man. Where you starting today?"

Lucas surveyed the lot. All around him, customer cars were being pulled into service bays for routine maintenance, oil changes, tire rotations, and a few for more serious work. Gahan Motors occupied more than three miles of prime real estate directly off I-81. It was comprised of several dealerships; Toyota, Mitsubishi, Honda, Nissan, Dodge, Chrysler, Chevrolet, Ford, Kia, Subaru, Mercedes, and BMW all operated under the Gahan umbrella.

Wayne Gahan and Gahan Motors employed hundreds of salespeople, along with mechanics, technicians, IT specialists, marketing experts, accountants, legal services, security, office managers, and secretaries. A veritable army of support was necessary to keep the Gahan Motors machine in motion. The only other organizations that came close to supporting as many livelihoods in Summit County were the government or the Volvo truck factory.

Lucas burned at not being put in a managerial or at least a salesman role.

Sales jobs at Gahan Motors were highly coveted as they were the stars of the show and treated to higher salaries and better benefits. Lucas had never wanted to work here. He thought he'd be playing professional ball, but since he was stuck, he wanted a top job. It was, after all, his birthright. Wayne wouldn't be where he was without Julia, and Lucas knew it. His last name was on every paycheck issued! It wasn't fair.

"Come on, man. These cars ain't gonna wash themselves," Brandon said.

"Yeah. Fuck this job." Lucas grabbed his bucket and headed out to the lot.

"Excuse me, sir? We need some help."

Lucas looked over his shoulder from where he was crouched down, scrubbing the tires of a Honda Accord. He considered telling the person to fuck off until he saw the legs. Smooth, firm, and sexy, he followed them up to make eye contact with the owner. She was fine. Green eyes, seventeen or eighteen, figure both curvy and athletic, wavy auburn hair, and a splash of freckles across her nose.

Lucas turned on his most charming smile. "Yes, ma'am? How can I help?"

"Oh, don't call me ma'am. I'm Ciara. That's my dad over there." Ciara pointed to a middle-aged man wearing a blue button-up shirt and khaki pants looking in the window of a Nissan Sentra.

"I'm Lucas Gahan."

Ciara's eyes widened a little. She pointed to the name on the building. "As in...?"

"Guilty. My father is Wayne Gahan."

"Wow, I wouldn't have pictured the boss's son cleaning cars."

Bitch. "Well, there are no small jobs." Lucas smiled. "It all has to be done."

"Oh! I didn't mean it in a bad way. It's impressive, is all. I bet your father loves your work ethic." A flush rose to her cheeks.

"Interested in anything specific?" Lucas asked, taking a small step closer.

"We're looking at that Sentra."

"Is this for him? Or for you?"

Ciara smiled, brushing an errant strand of hair from her face. "For me. A combination graduation present and bribe."

"Go for the extras package. Take advantage." Lucas tipped her a wink.

She laughed. "Are you in college?"

"I'm taking a semester off. I wanted to rest and get some real-world experience."

"Oh Nice."

"I can always go back when I'm ready, no worries." The lie sliding smooth from his mouth. Lucas pivoted to stand beside her.

"Worry about what? The price of these cars?" a man asked.

Lucas looked away from Ciara's cleavage to make eye contact with her father. He'd approached them unnoticed while Lucas flirted. Undaunted, Lucas stepped forward with his hand out. "Lucas Gahan. Ciara here tells me you're bribing her with a car today."

Ciara's mouth dropped open.

"Did she now?" her father asked, losing his hostile glare.

"I suggested she take advantage and get the perks package." Lucas was enjoying himself. *Only men sell cars, right, Dad?* "This Accord gets great gas mileage, has an excellent collision rating, Bluetooth connectivity, eight-inch touch screen, a backup camera, and they maintain their value. For a first car, you could do a lot worse."

///

Lucas waved goodbye to Ciara as she turned off the lot in her new Accord with Lucas' number in her phone. Hot little piece, and he intended to find out all about her. He had her number, and she had his, and in a day or two, he'd text her under the guise of checking on the car.

He had to get Michelle, the sales manager, to send an actual salesman to handle the paperwork. Lucas wasn't certified to do that part. Commission wouldn't go to him either. That was all right. There were other compensations to be had, Lucas thought, watching the Accord speeding toward I-81.

///

Mark began his senior year by falling in love. She was new at school and had beautiful green eyes and thick auburn hair. Mark ached when he looked at her. Simultaneously hot and cold, his palms sweat, and his stomach flopped like he was about to vomit. She sat next to him in homeroom, where they waited to get their schedules. Mark could smell her shampoo—something flowery—and the clean soapy scent of her skin. It made him light-headed. His mouth felt full of cotton.

"Excuse me, do you know where these classes are?" she asked, leaning over to hand him her schedule.

Mark's heart picked up, pounding in his ears. "Uh, looks like we have classes together. I'm Governor's

School too. We go to a separate building with the rest of the gifted kids. I can walk you over there after homeroom."

"Governor's School isn't in this building?" she asked.

"No, they keep the nerds separate." Mark tried for a casual chuckle, but his face was flaming hot.

"Are you alright?" she asked.

"You're hot." Mark gulped in horror. "I mean, aren't you hot?" If possible, his face flushed even hotter.

She laughed. "Thanks! You're hot too."

Mark stared. Clearly, she enjoyed his discomfort. Mark didn't know how to reply. *Could I be more awkward?*

The bell rang, announcing the end of class. "Saved by the bell," she said. "But not really."

"I'm Mark," he managed. "Mark Branton."

"Nice to meet you, Mark Branton. I'm Ciara Aleman." Her hand was soft and warm as he shook it. "So, where's this other building at?"

Mark's feet never hit the ground on the walk to the Governor's School. Floating along beside the most beautiful girl he'd ever seen, Mark felt like his chest might burst.

As they crossed the parking lot, Mark noticed Albert Foster's beat-up Outback. *Hard to believe it's only three years old*, Mark thought. The sides were dented and scratched. A spiderweb crack ran across the windshield, matching another on the rear windshield. The antenna had been bent and straightened so often it resembled a bolt of lightning. One end of the rear bumper was held up with yellow nylon rope. Burns dotted the car like a strange pox.

Mark knew Alicia was responsible. She hated that car for some reason.

Alicia walked ahead of them—also heading for the Governor's School—dressed in black from head to toe. She'd dyed her hair such a deep purple that it, too, appeared black until the sun hit it just right. She veered off the sidewalk, pulling a screwdriver from her shoulder bag. She dragged the screwdriver down the length of the driver's side, then put the screwdriver back in her bag. Turning her head, she saw Mark, waved, and continued, never breaking stride.

"What was that about?" Ciara asked, a small furrow forming between her eyebrows.

"What can I say? She hates that car."

"Does she do that to other cars?"

"No. She leaves other people's property alone. Alicia—that's her name—only vandalizes her father's car."

"Her father works here?"

"Yeah. Albert Foster is a custodian. About my height but fat, kind of hunched, mumbles to himself."

"Haven't seen him yet. My dad just bought me a new car, and I don't want her messing with it. Why does she do that?"

"I'm not sure."

"You seem to know a lot about her. Former girlfriend?"

Mark shook his head with vigor. "No! Um, we were friends in elementary school, and we played Warcraft together up until freshmen year."

"What happened freshmen year?"

"I'm not sure. There were rumors, not worth repeating, but she didn't log on anymore. Started dressing in black, being mean. I tried to keep her as a friend, but she wasn't interested."

"That's kind of sad. I wonder what made her so angry."

"You could ask her."

"Sure, I'll just walk up to a complete stranger and ask, 'Hey there! Why are you so mad?' It'll go over well, I'm sure."

"Well, when you put it like that..."

They didn't speak about Lucas or the upcoming party again. Mark didn't like it, but he was powerless to stop her. He'd meant what he said; he didn't think it was a good idea. A worse idea would be for him to try to force his will. Ciara wasn't the kind of girl who'd appreciate a bossy man telling her what to do. She'd probably bounce his head off the dashboard before tossing him out of her moving car.

It wasn't Mark's nature to tell people what to do anyway. His desire to protect Ciara came from a good place, but she'd never asked for his protection. Forcing it on her could push her away. That said, Lucas *was* bad news. While Mark was still unaware of the details of his date with Alicia three years ago, the aftermath was undeniable.

Mark had tried to force himself into Alicia's life as well.

But Alicia changed. Pushed him away. Resented his interference. Filled with wrath, she used her anger to keep the world away. Even to keep her own father away. There were rumors—in a small town, there always were—that what happened to Alicia went beyond bad and into nightmare territory. The thought of a similar event happening to Ciara made Mark sick with worry.

He needed to know what happened to Alicia. Only two people, Lucas and Alicia, knew the real story. Neither were talking to him. He'd heard she spent most of her time at the Colony now. Another trip out there might be in order. Lexi seemed to like him the last time they spoke, and she still waved if she saw him walking to school or heading home from work. Maybe she could help.

We can help, little brother.

Two weeks passed. Fall took full reign as summer slunk away for another year. October brought about pumpkins, hayrides, corn mazes, and Halloween hype. A wet spring led to a brilliant fall. The wind, sharp with winter coming, blew through trees colored in vibrant red, orange, and yellow foliage.

A colder wind blew in Mark's heart.

He did his best to hide his worry for Ciara. They talked, joked, grew closer, and Mark thought on at least one occasion that she would have permitted him to kiss her. He'd chickened out. Inexperience with women crippled his confidence. Confused about the fear he felt, both for her and of her, Mark tried to take the advice reptile often whispered: *Be calm. Be still.*

Einar remained his enigmatic self. Often coming and going for reasons known only to himself. On weekends, they'd often met at Coopers Cave to take flights together or hunt, but Einar seemed to be distancing himself from the reptile. In earlier days, they would hang around the campfire, and Einar would speak of the stones, their song, historical lycanthropes, and things legends got wrong.

The term lycanthropy is often associated with wolves, thanks to Hollywood. Specifically, human transformation into *Canis lupus*. According to Einar, wolves were the most common, followed by bear, but in actuality, a lycanthrope simply transformed into an animal spirit, not just wolves or bears. Einar said their kind—those who heard the song, picked by the stone—were far more common than Mark believed.

"Wolves are everywhere. It won't be long, and you'll be able to smell them. Filthy animals, really. You'll be amazed you never noticed them before. Stink to high heaven. Worse than rats, which are surprisingly good company," Einar had said once, poking at the fire with a stick, watching the sparks dance on the breeze.

"Bears are almost as common. Fiery temper on a bear. Piss a bear off at your peril. I saw a bear get into a bar fight. He didn't transform—didn't need to—and still punched a man's jaw off. Horrible mess, people puking everywhere. There weren't enough cops in the town to arrest him. They piled on, and he tossed them around. Finally, they quit trying and let him go with a promise to not come back. Or maybe he let them go... I don't quite remember. Hell of a thing, Mark, hell of a thing. Don't anger bears."

Einar would float from topic to topic, like a butterfly after nectar. A sip here, a taste there, never getting too deep into any one thing lest he leave himself exposed. Mark enjoyed listening to his rambling. Knowing there were others in the world like him was soothing.

But Einar seemed to grow uncomfortable around the reptile. The conversation had dried up, and Einar became sullen, moody. Was Einar afraid of the reptile? Why? He didn't know and supposed it didn't matter. The end results were the same, Einar wasn't around as much and Mark found himself missing those conversations. Missing the intimacy of speaking about this new part of himself to someone like him.

Mark liked being Mark, but he was beginning to love being the reptile. A dormant power lay within him. He'd dipped his toe into deep waters, but he couldn't say what miracles or monsters swam the depths. The reptile had said the spirit within magnified with contact with the Song. Not entirely sure what that meant, Mark liked to believe the reptile multiplied his better character traits.

Mark was always in control and always remembered the time spent flying, hunting, bounding tree to tree, relishing the newfound strength and agility his body possessed, as well as the acute disappointment he felt at leaving his glorious form to return to his small pink body.

As for the savage joy he felt hunting, the primal ecstasy of tearing through the sounder, that disturbed him in a way hard to quantify. Mark didn't enjoy the thought of such savagery being a part of his nature. It felt like finding out vipers nested underneath the bed.

Mark called Millie and begged off work for the evening. Millie didn't mind, only asked if Mark felt okay.

"Yeah, I'm fine. There's a personal matter I need to attend to. If it runs late, I don't want you waiting around for me. I'll square things away in the morning."

"Anything I can do to help?" Millie asked. "Need a ride somewhere?"

"No, thank you, sir. I'm good."

"No problem, Mark. You're a good boy. If you need tomorrow as well, leave a message on the machine. It'll be fine."

"No worries. I'll be in tomorrow morning early. And I'll get the hospital shipment ready before I go to school."

"That pretty girl gonna pick you up?"

"I sure hope so."

"You hang on to her. She's a good'un."

"Yes, sir."

"Boy, we've known each other for over three years. Long enough for you to stop calling me sir every time we speak. Call me Millie, like the rest of Summit Valley does."

"Yes, sir."

Getting away from Ciara proved more difficult. She wanted to go with him, and Mark didn't have a good reason for her not to. She said she'd drive him wherever he needed to go and lying to her felt wrong. A lie of omission, however, felt forgivable. Justifiable, even.

Something wrong happened to people at the Colony. Mark still had nightmares about the way everyone had stopped moving and stared at him when he'd interrupted Lexi three years ago. Mark didn't want Ciara exposed to whatever preyed upon the people there. Protecting her from herself, even if she didn't understand what he was trying to shield her from, was the right call. *Hell, I don't understand what's going on there,* Mark thought. The reptile agreed, whispering its approval as Mark ducked and dodged Ciara's frustration with his sudden obstinance.

"Are you going to run all the way out there? It's like ten miles or something."

"I thought I'd walk, actually."

"Actually," Ciara mocked his tone before resuming her argument, "taking off work for a twenty-mile hike is stupid when you have a ride. We can go up there together. Then you can do whatever it is you feel you need to do, and we can go grab some dinner afterward. I'd like a date before this party, which I really don't want to go to anymore."

"Good. Don't go."

"Let's make an evening of it. We can go to the movies in Nilbud. This early in the week, I bet we'll have the theatre to ourselves." Ciara made it hard to argue. She wasn't going to give an inch. Everything she said made sense. "If you walk round trip, that's going to take all night. My way, we get things done and get to spend some time together."

Mark quickly realized she was not one to be dissuaded. Ciara had a stubbornness he couldn't deny. She'd made up her mind, and the best Mark could do was hope she stayed in the car.

"Okay. We'll go together. But Alicia doesn't know you and isn't thrilled with me. I need to talk to her by myself."

"See how much easier this is when you listen?" Ciara smiled.

"I'm serious. I need to talk to her alone." Mark doubted Alicia would tell him about her date with Lucas. He was certain she wouldn't do it in front of a stranger. This was something he had to do, had to know, in order to protect Ciara from a monster.

"Fine. You talk to her. Alone." Ciara made a face. "Then we go to dinner. Until then, I'll be a good girl and wait in the car."

Ciara pulled into the gravel bordering Colony Road. Mark knew could have run here faster—and flown faster still—but Ciara would've thought him certifiable. Telling your prospective girlfriend you turn into a dragon just wasn't done.

"Wait here. I'll be back soon."

Ciara saluted. "Yes, sir!"

"Smartass."

Mark passed the security booth without a glance. He ran into William, who had bucket and brush in hand.

"Do it again, she said. Paint the fence. The whole fence. Not good enough, so do it again."

Knowing the outcome, Mark made no effort to speak to him. Plus, Lexi was in the main building waiting for him. He didn't know how he was able to feel Lexi's impatience, but Mark knew he was right, and he fought the urge to hurry to her.

Patience, little brother. Danger.

"I know. This place isn't right."

I'll be close.

"Glad to hear it."

The lack of activity on the grounds disturbed Mark. Last time, the Colony grounds had pulsed with organized chaos. Back on that pleasant fall day, even with the threat of a storm looming, the ladies of the Colony had been out painting, talking, exercising, reading, and working. The air had hummed with activity. But today, other than the fence painter, William, Mark hadn't seen anyone. The grounds around him were quiet, still.

Wind rustled the leaves, which scraped along the ground, hissing and whispering their warnings. Branches swayed as if waving him back. Leave this place, the trees seemed to say. Turn around! Run! Flee! The silent menace all around him made his thighs tighten and his balls draw up. Mark wanted to turn his back to the wind and run as fast as he could back to Ciara.

Ciara.

The only reason he came back here was for her. Mark fought the anxiety that assailed him like a physical force. Pushing himself to move one foot in front of the other, he kept her face in mind. He needed to know what awaited her a few short days away. Mark wouldn't let whatever happened to Alicia happen to her.

The Colony had grown in the last three years. The main compound remained the same, the large central dome still the dominant feature, but the smaller pods around the central dome had multiplied. Spreading out in equal measure along either side of the main entrance, the Colony resembled a cluster of giant white grapes laid in the middle of a green field.

Or a giant hive.

No architecture in Summit Valley came anywhere near the rolling monstrosity the Colony had become. Another feature, which took Mark a minute to recognize—there weren't any windows. Other than the glass of the main entrance—two sliding doors—Mark couldn't pinpoint anywhere else someone might look outside.

No one could look in either.

Mark pushed himself forward, the anxiety lessening the closer he got to the building, as if the force pushing against him recognized he wasn't going to stop. Whatever the reason, Mark felt some semblance of relief, and his stride became more natural.

The double doors slid open with a blast of cool preconditioned neutral industrial air. A reception desk dominated the lobby. With no one there to greet him, the lobby was as silent as the grounds. A folded note was propped at the center of the desk, MARK written in black letters across the front.

Picking up the note, Mark looked around. Natural light filtered in from above, lending a surprising amount of warmth to the lobby. Unsuccessful in his attempts to deduce exactly how the light filtered in, Mark turned his attention back to the note bearing his name. Fresh ink smudged onto his fingers as he opened the note.

Mr. Branton,

Since you are determined to visit, please come to my office. The entrance is to your left. Alicia will show you the way.

−Lexi

Mark looked up to see Alicia standing behind the reception desk, watching him.

"Jesus, Alicia! You scared me! Were you hiding back there?"

"Nope. Come on. She wants to see you."

"Seriously, where did you come from?"

Instead of answering, Alicia came out from behind the desk and held open a door. Eyebrows raised, she motioned for him to precede her. "After you, sir."

The contempt in her tone wasn't lost on him.

She led him through a confusing maze of narrow hallways. Mark lost count of the number of turns they took. Close and claustrophobic in width, the hallways rose to unusual heights. At six feet two, Mark was used to not having much headspace most places he went. The ceiling towered over him, at least twenty feet high, but if another person came from the opposite direction, Mark would have had to fall in behind Alicia because the walls pressed in that close.

While Mark had the sense the place was packed with people, he didn't see anyone. They passed a daycare—empty—and offices—also empty. Bare dorm-style rooms, which Mark would have sworn seemed to be buzzing seconds before, stood abandoned. The beds were neatly made, everything clean, orderly, and in place. The thin hallway carpet even ate the sound of their footsteps. It was like the building had frozen one second before an explosion. Mark felt as though he were walking through the eye of a hurricane.

Alicia stopped before a door marked DIRECTOR. "Here ya go, killer. Be polite. I'll wait here."

"Thanks."

It was the most she'd spoken to him in years.

Mark knocked on the door as he opened it.

"Come in, Mark." Lexi sat behind a large corner desk. Two monitors blocked most of her face. After finishing up whatever she'd been typing, she slid over for an unobstructed view of him. "My, you've grown up. Not a scared little boy anymore, are you? Still looking to save the maiden fair?"

"I guess not. I didn't do so hot a job on the last one."

"I disagree. You brought her to my attention. We have helped Alicia through some trying times. I wouldn't have found her if not for you."

"Doesn't seem like she's better..."

"There's a lot for her to unpack."

"Which is kind of why I'm here."

"How can I help?" Lexi leaned forward, hands folded atop the desk. Smart and professional, she intimidated him for some reason. Lexi made him feel small, transparent, like all his secrets were laid bare.

"I'd like to speak with Alicia," he said.

"You don't need my permission."

"I know, but I didn't want to—"

"What? Barge in unannounced and uninvited?" She raised a brow.

"I know I wasn't invited—"

"Mr. Branton, you know what we do here." It wasn't a question.

"I only wanted to speak with Alicia. What you do here isn't my business."

"On that, we agree. I tolerated your intrusion last time because I understood you had feelings for her. You came from a good place. But now, you want something else, something you aren't entitled to, and I'm afraid I won't tolerate the intrusion. Not here. Not now."

Let me, little brother.

The reptile came forth suddenly. Mark's eyes blazed, piercing Lexi in place with the intensity of his gaze. She froze in the act of standing up, unable to look away. The reptile trapped Lexi's mind, drowning her consciousness in a pool of silver light, stripping her resolve away. He spoke in her head, soothing her, belying her fears.

Calm, Lexi. We will speak to the girl. No one will hurt her. You don't mind.

"Speak to her. She's waiting outside the door," Lexi said.

Go get her. Find something else to do. Little brother will have his talk. We will go. Your nest remains unharmed. All remains well. Be calm.

"Well, I am extremely busy this time of year," Lexi said. "Have your talk and try not to disturb my patient. She's been through more than you know."

Ciara was in two of Mark's classes, and they had the same lunch.

"Any plans for lunch?" she asked him.

"I thought about joining Alicia for a stomp on the Subaru, but I think she made other plans."

Ciara punched him in the shoulder. "Ha-ha. Too cool to be seen having lunch with the new girl, huh?"

Mark's face flushed. "Well, I suppose I might condescend to make time."

"Good. You're the only person I know here, and I'd hate to have to kick your ass."

Mark thought having his ass kicked by Ciara wouldn't be the worst thing in the world.

"I don't know... I'm skinny, but I'm wiry. Wiry and tough like old boot leather. But much better looking, of course. Besides, do you want to risk tarnishing your reputation being seen with me? I'm kind of a loser."

"Since I have no reputation, I'm willing to risk it. But understand, once I'm queen of the school, I'll pretend not to know you."

"I'd expect no less," Mark said.

"Good. You won't be disappointed, then. Let's get lunch, loser."

After school, Mark headed for National Linen. He'd promised Millie he'd knock out the rest of the morning's shipment that he'd left on pallets before school. Over the years, Mark had earned enough trust that Millie let him come and go. And now that Mark was of legal age, Millie had him on the payroll—nice and above board.

Mark could have made the trip in a few short minutes, but he didn't like putting on displays in broad daylight. Einar encouraged him in his caution. People were panicky. Besides, Mark wanted to replay every second with Ciara over in his head. He swore he could still smell her shampoo.

A gray Accord pulled up beside him and honked, startling Mark out of his daydreams. He stumbled and fell on his butt. Mark heard her high sweet laughter before he saw her.

"Hey, handsome! Want a ride?"

Mark stood back up, dusting grass off his hind parts. "Sure."

"You all right? Sorry I scared you."

"I wasn't scared. I was daydreaming."

"About me?" A car honked behind Ciara. "Saved by the bell—again. Get in! I'm holding up traffic."

Mark hustled around and got in.

The heavy after-school traffic on Pico honked irritably. Ciara ignored the hostile looks from other drivers and coasted to the intersection with Route 11. "Where are we headed?"

"Take a left and head downtown, or what's left of it."

"Some fire, huh?"

"It was. Mom and I weren't in town at the time. When we were allowed back, everything was gone."

"That's terrible. Did you lose your dad in the fire?"

Mark shook his head. "He was a soldier. He died in Iraq."

"Jesus, Mark, I'm sorry. I can't stay away from sore spots."

She seemed genuine, and Mark didn't mind. "It's all right. We're doing great. Better now. Take a left on Washington."

Ciara turned on her blinker and moved into the turn lane. The arrow was red. Cars heading straight passed by, mean mugging her for holding them up. Neither Mark nor Ciara noticed or cared. Mark felt like he was alone in the universe with the most amazing person he'd ever met.

"We're making another left right down here. See that big white building?"

"You have a job?"

"I do some part-time work in the warehouse here and at another spot closer to home."

"Two jobs?"

He nodded. "I mow lawns in the summer too."

"Do you leave any work for anyone else?"

"It's not that big a deal. I push a broom around part time. Pick this up, set it down over there. Not exactly a career at NASA."

Ciara cocked her head. "Is that what you want?"

"Not at the moment."

She smiled, made the left, and dropped him in the parking lot. "What time do you get off work?"

Mark leaned down, propping himself in the open door. "I shouldn't be more than an hour here."

"No set schedules?"

"Nah. Millie doesn't care so long as the work gets done. Once I'm finished, I can leave. I did most of it before school this morning."

"Don't you sleep?"

"Not much."

Mark couldn't keep the grin off his face. Millie asked about the pretty girl who'd dropped him off, and his flaming cheeks told Millie everything he needed to know. An hour later, Mark left the warehouse.

Waiting in the parking lot with a drink from Sonic was Ciara. "I'm not stalking you, really."

"I don't think I'd mind you stalking me."

Ciara's face flushed this time. She handed him the drink. "I got a snack from Sonic and thought you might like a drink after work. If you're not sick of me yet."

"A drink sounds great. What is it?"

"Vanilla Dr. Pepper."

"Dr. Pepper comes in vanilla?"

"Sonic will put a squirt of vanilla flavor into any drink. I like these."

Mark accepted the large foam cup and took a drink through the red plastic straw.

"How is it?" she asked.

"Sweet."

She looked upset. "You don't like it?"

"It's delicious. I've never had anything like it."

Ciara grinned. "Liar."

"I'm not! It's amazing. Thank you."

A sparrow landed on Mark's shoulder and cocked its little head.

"Oh my God! A bird just landed on your shoulder!"

"Yeah, this little guy is my friend. I nursed him back to health after he was hit by a car. Since then, he kind of follows me around. This is really good." Mark shook the cup, and the sparrow flew off.

"Amazing…" Ciara watched the bird alight on an electrical wire across the street, then pulled her gaze back to Mark. "I'm glad you like it. It's a thank-you for putting up with me today. I'm not normally so clingy, but I feel comfortable around you." She looked away, cheeks pink. "I'm talking too much."

"I'm just waiting on you to get sick of me. I'm not a popular guy."

"Maybe tomorrow."

"Good enough."

She laughed again. Mark decided he'd do just about anything to hear her laugh. He'd only known her a few short hours, but he knew he was in love.

"Want a ride home?" Ciara twirled her key around her finger.

"A vanilla Dr. Pepper and a ride home? Best. Day. Ever."

Ciara wasn't lying; she did feel comfortable around Mark. Safe. Though she didn't know him well enough to justify her feelings out loud. There was something about him though. He was cute, and working in a warehouse had done good things for his chest and arms, but what she felt went deeper than animal magnetism. There was a gentleness to Mark, a sweetness she didn't usually see in boys her age.

She knew he liked her. His face flushed every time she spoke to him. But even his awkwardness appealed to her. She hummed along with the radio as she drove, happy her father took the job here and brought her to Mark. Of course, he'd probably move them back to Summerville if he knew she'd already met a boy.

She pulled into her driveway and parked beside her father's Dodge Ram. Ciara loved the truck; its blend of old-world style and modern technology suited her father perfectly. Tough and dependable with a bit of hidden flare, just like her daddy. He was an IT professional, an ex-soldier, a software engineer, who liked old blues artists and documentaries about World War II.

Her phone buzzed.

How's the car? read the message from the cute sales guy.

She dropped the phone in her pocket and went inside.

Her mother took one look at her and asked, "What's his name?"

"Whose name?" Ciara asked, unable to hide her blush or her smile.

"Uh-huh. Don't say anything to your father. I just got us unpacked."

"What's her name?" Sabrina asked.

"Whose name?" Mark tried his best to appear innocent.

"Right. You know, son, we've met. You've been floating around the house since you got home. You're fooling no one."

Mark sighed, then smiled. "Ciara. Her name is Ciara."

"Does Ciara have a last name?"

"Aleman."

"Pretty."

"She is."

"I meant her name."

"That too."

His mom raised a brow. "She the one who dropped you off this afternoon?"

"Yeah."

"Oh my Lord, is my little boy in love?"

"I'm not a little boy. And I'm not—uh, I don't know. She's incredible, Mom. I've never seen anyone like her. Her dad transferred here from South Carolina to assist the truck plant. I love Volvo. We should get a Volvo."

"So, her dad works at Volvo and Miss Aleman has stolen my baby's heart... That's it. I need to meet this heifer, see what she's about, check her teeth."

More than a little nervous at the thought of his mother meeting Ciara, Mark broke contact and went to his room. Bone followed him upstairs and lay down on Mark's pillow while Mark sat in the middle of his room staring at the posters on his walls, restless. Comic book heroes were gradually being replaced by band and movie posters to reflect Mark's maturing tastes. He'd snagged a poster from Dollar Tree of a movie called *Frankenstein Unbound*. Mark had never seen the movie, but he liked the picture.

An iris stitched together from parts of a brown eye, a green one, and a blue stared out between the words Frankenstein and Unbound. Along the bottom was the film's R rating, along with credits in smaller print.

Mark just liked the creepy stitched eyeball. Maybe his tastes weren't as mature as he'd have liked to believe.

Be calm, little brother.

The thought came from nowhere. Startled, Mark looked around to make sure he was still alone.

You'll never be alone, little brother. I am with you.

"Hello?" Mark asked. A time existed not so long ago, when Mark might have found a voice in his head strange. That time was long gone. Since his first accidental transformation in school, Mark had become a connoisseur of oddities.

"Are you...the reptile?"

We are. Go to the mirror.

"Who is *we*?" Mark asked while heading over to the full-length mirror on the back of his door. "Oh."

Mark's reflection answered his question. A phantom reptile hovered around Mark in the mirror. Its serpentine neck curled around his shoulders so it could whisper in his ear. Crouched on hind legs, wings tucked, the reptile held Mark to its silver chest. A black-and-silver tail wrapped in front of Mark's feet.

We are one, little brother. You and me.

"Why couldn't I hear you or see you before?"

Bond takes time.

"Are there others out there like us?"

None like us. The reptile in the mirror shook its head. *Hearts are different. Wolves, wasps, different.*

"I don't understand."

Wait.

"Then now what? What do we do?"

Be calm. Be still.

"How did this happen? I mean, how did we happen?"

Felt you, little brother, in the void. The stones sang. We answered.

"Einar says we give life to the spirits of the stones. They, in turn, give power."

Deceiver. Trickster.

"Einar?"

Deceiver. Black heart.

Ciara Aleman lay on her bed conflicted. The salesman, Lucas, had invited her to a party still a few weeks out, claiming he still helped the football team out and would be happy to introduce her to a few people at Summit Valley High. She'd meet other students who didn't go to the Governor's School. Part of her wanted to believe his interest in her was friendly, but she knew better. As nice as he was—charming, even—something about him made her skin crawl.

Being alone with him wasn't something she cared to do.

Besides, Mark seemed...interesting, even if he wasn't popular. Guys who cared rarely were, in her experience. Her mother thought she should go, enjoy, and not commit herself. Dad didn't know. Shannon, her bestie in Summerville, thought she should go too. Cute older guy—why not? Ciara found it difficult to explain the general creepiness she sensed. Lucas never did anything overt, and she didn't even really know him. Still, the feeling of yuck remained.

Bad, bad, icky, bad, bad.

Perhaps she was overreacting. Seeing phantoms where there were none. She wasn't using her interest in Mark as an excuse not to make friends, was she? Was she looking for a convenient reason to remain relatively isolated and alone? She was angry at her father for leaving Summerville. Her senior year should have been the greatest year of her life. Instead, she found herself in a strange town and virtually friendless.

But blaming Dad wasn't fair, and she knew it. It was a good thing for him, and in turn, her family. Her new car was proof enough. She decided she would make the best of it. Besides, what could be so bad about going to a party? It was just one night.

She sent Lucas a text saying it sounded like fun.

Ciara surprised Mark Monday morning. He opened the door to find her pulling into the driveway. Mark waved and met her coming up the driveway. She'd brought coffee and bagels from Chuck's on First.

"Thought you might like a ride to school," she said.

He grinned. "I'd love one. Coffee smells great."

"I got you one too."

Mark opened the passenger door to the smell of new car, hot coffee, fresh bread, and Ciara's floral shampoo—a not unpleasant mixture that made Mark delightfully light-headed. Tossing his backpack in the rear, Mark pointed at the bag of bagels. "Can I have one of those too? I love blueberry."

"How do you know there's a blueberry bagel in there?"

"I can smell it."

"You're kidding," Ciara said.

Careful, little brother.

Mark forced a chuckle. "Lucky guess?"

The skeptical look on her face—specifically the cute wrinkle between her eyebrows—told him Ciara didn't buy it, but she just said, "Well, you were right. I got you a blueberry bagel."

Mark wasted no time opening the bag. "Can I eat in here? Do you mind?"

"No, you have to sit there smelling it all the way to school." She laughed at the sullen look on his face. "I'm kidding. Of course you can eat in the car. I got it for you!"

Mark stuck his hand in the bag. "I didn't want to be rude. My dad didn't like people eating in the car. He used to get all bent out of shape about it." He pulled the bagel and a tiny square of cream cheese wrapped in foil out of the bag. Using the paper bag as a tray, Mark smeared the cream cheese, slapped the halves together, and took a bite.

Ciara grinned. "I've never seen anyone mash cream cheese into such a perfectly even layer before."

Mark washed down the bite with a bit of coffee. "I was hungry. Tastes amazing."

Ciara turned north on Washington. Downtown Summit Valley was waking up. The sun burned the remaining morning fog off the streets like coffee burned away sleepiness. Traffic, while still light at the early hour, picked up. People were coming to life all around.

Summer still held sway during the day, but fall let its coming presence be felt during the cool mornings and nights. Trees, while still green, were gradually being infiltrated by spots of yellow and orange. Mark sat beside a beautiful girl on an amazing day, feeling happy and blessed to be alive. He didn't understand why she'd picked him, but at that moment, he didn't care.

"Mark, can I ask you something?"

"Sure."

"I got invited to a party. I think I'm going to go."

The bagel turned to a bowling ball in Mark's stomach. He tried to remain nonchalant and keep the concern out of his tone—and the jealousy out of his voice. "Who with?"

"The guy who sold us this car. He said he does work with the football team and knows people—seniors—at school."

Relief swept through Mark. A car salesman? He didn't have anything to worry about. It wasn't like Mark had any claim on Ciara, but he felt there might be something happening between them, and he was confident Ciara felt the same way.

"Nice. Here we go... You're going to meet all the cool kids, and I'll go back to bagel-less mornings."

"Aw." Ciara pressed her bottom lip out in a faux pout.

Mark smirked. "Who's the guy?"

"He's the son of the owner of Gahan Motors. Name's Lucas. Know him?"

The bowling ball came hurling back as though thrown by a giant. Mark thought for an awful moment that he might get sick. He cleared his throat. "We've met."

Ciara glanced over at him. "You look sick. Everything okay?"

Mark gripped the door handle, placing his forehead against the cool window glass. He knew a girl who went on a date with Lucas. Sure, he did. And she was never the same after that. Mark didn't know how to warn Ciara away without sounding petty. Washington Street slid by, turning into Fifth.

"Yeah, I'm okay. I just…felt a little queasy for a moment there. Must not be getting enough sleep."

"You turned a little green when I mentioned Lucas."

"Yeah, sorry." Mark went quiet for a beat. "Look, Ciara, I'll be honest with you—"

"Uh-oh."

"I'm not super excited at the thought of you going anywhere with Lucas Gahan. I've heard bad things about him." Seeing her about to protest, Mark held up a hand. "But I'm no one to tell you where to go or who to go with. If you want to go to the party, all I can say is, I hope you have fun and please be careful."

"Mark Branton, are you jealous?"

"A little."

Ciara pulled into a parking space at school and slid the transmission into park. "You don't have to worry."

"Of course not. You brought me the bagel."

"And coffee."

"And a vanilla Dr. Pepper."

"Which you hated."

"Not true." Mark grinned and pushed the car door open. "Come on, let's go."

Alicia came in, confused with Lexi's departure. Mark turned, his eyes shining like molten silver, trapping her in his gaze. "Sit down, Alicia. I need to speak to you."

"A-About what?" she asked, unable to look away. As she stumbled around the desk, she bumped her hip hard enough to rock the monitors.

"Careful. Don't hurt yourself," Mark said softly.

She sat, and the chair groaned, accepting her weight as the strength left her legs. She wasn't afraid. Peace radiated from Mark and wrapped her in a warm secure blanket. Her hip throbbed, but the pain was muted and far away, a radio broadcast playing low in another room.

His eyes were moonlit pools of deep still water. She wanted to lose herself in the depths. She felt light, floating, intangible. A sensation of calm and weightlessness filled her. Alicia was a little girl again. Wrapped in her mother's arms, smelling her clean skin, safe. Her father wrapped his arms around her mother, Alicia held snug between them, her father strong and firm, and her mother soft and gentle, both fierce in their love for her.

Hold that memory, child. We will be through soon.

A voice whispered to her about that night.

No... She didn't want to think about that, about them. She wanted to stay here between her parents. Safe and loved. Her mother alive, holding her close. Her father still loving her, believing her, not selling her for a car. Not trading her dignity and self-respect to pay the hospital and therapy bills that would pile up for years.

///

The reptile guided Mark. Together, they stepped into Alicia's mind. The reptile held her in a cherished memory of her parents. Mark followed the pain throbbing in her hip. Pain had become a central part of Alicia's life. For three years, she'd sunk further into a deepening quagmire of depression and hurt as the pain burned out the core of her.

The physical pain of her bruised hip led the way. One pain led to another. Soon, Mark found himself looking through her eyes. Fourteen years old, both scared and excited—

—because he'd be there any minute! She'd spent the afternoon picking out the right outfit. Evidence of the search piled on the floor around her bed. She'd kept her makeup to just a touch around the eyes because Daddy wouldn't let her go if she used too much. "You look like you're ready to attack the war wagon!" he'd yell, full of indignation. "Go wash your face before I scrub it with a Brillo pad!"

A knock at the door brought her to her feet. She ran over to her window, which looked down on their street. The back of his red Mustang, visible from her vantage point, brought a flare of color to their drab building. Dad tried his best, but they'd never afford something like that. Riding in it made her feel special, deserving.

"Alicia!" her father called from the living room. "Your friend is here!"

Shyness descended on butterfly wings, flitting across her thighs, up to her chest and shortening her breath, making her heart pound and her nipples erect, then finally settling in her stomach. Deliciously light-headed, she left the bathroom after one final check of her makeup and went downstairs.

An incredible sadness washed through Mark as he traveled through Alicia's memory. She'd been so excited, believing Lucas cared for her, wanted to be with her. She'd felt her world turning around, but Mark knew her dream evening ended with horrible life-altering consequence. He wanted to scream at her not to go, but he'd become a passenger on a train to hell, knowing the destination and powerless to stop it. His only option was to ride it out and see what she had to show him.

Lucas ran a finger up Alicia's leg as she put on her seat belt.

"Lucas! We're still in the driveway!"

"Baby, I can't help it. You're so sexy."

A flush raced through her. He was sexy—even white teeth, T-shirt clinging to his muscular chest and shoulders, intoxicating cologne. She could die! Lucas kissed her at every stop light, rubbing his hands over her legs and stomach, using his thumb to touch her breasts while both pretended he wasn't doing exactly that. Her heart could've exploded from happiness.

Still, she wished he wasn't quite so handsy.

Alicia pushed the thought away. He couldn't help himself. He loved her, and she thought she might be falling in love with him. Lucas drove fast, making the engine scream. At every green light, he stomped the accelerator and made the tires chirp.

Lucas pulled a joint from the center console. "Let's get the party started a little early."

Nervous, Alicia took a small hit of the fragrant smoke, mimicking him.

"There you go, baby. Hold it in," Lucas encouraged.

It burned her throat and made her cough, but the joint soon relaxed her, soothing away any anxiety she felt riding with the top down while smoking marijuana. Lucas's hands on her body weren't bothering her as much either. In fact, his hand high on her thigh felt good—strong and warm. Every time she looked over at him, he was watching her. Smiling.

She was safe. It was okay. Lucas wouldn't let anything happen to her.

They drove into the country. She wasn't sure where. The mountains crowded close around them, trees creating dappled shadows on the twisting road. Eventually, they arrived at a driveway. Alicia saw nothing to indicate a party. A closed gated blocked vehicle traffic with a slotted grate on the ground beneath. Lucas got out and opened the gate barring their way.

"What's that?" Alicia asked.

"Cattle guard. Keeps the cows from wandering out. They won't walk on the grate." Lucas hopped back in. He was so knowledgeable! He always had the answer.

Lucas drove through, then got out and closed the gate behind them before continuing up the driveway. The gravel drive deteriorated into a pair of pothole-studded ruts. Lucas even took his hand off her thigh to put both on the wheel. To avoid scraping the bottom of the low-seated sports car, he was often forced off the trail to one side or the other until their path smoothed out in a big green lawn.

A large farmhouse with wraparound porches on the first and second floors dominated the clearing. An aging barn complete with a rusted roof decayed off to the right of the house. Lucas guided the Mustang toward the barn where other cars were parked. Students from Summit Valley High swarmed the grounds. Alicia recognized most of the people, even if only by face.

Everyone knew Lucas.

Several guys from the football team drank beer on the porch upstairs. They hooted greetings to Lucas as the pair crossed the yard.

"Hey, Gahan! What you got there?"

"Nice ride, Lucas! Can't wait!"

"Fish, baby! Love some fresh fish!"

"She's prepped and ready to go, too!" Lucas called back.

There were others there Alicia didn't know—older people, college age, watching with indifferent expressions. Alicia's fear spiked slightly as she realized the party was almost exclusively male. Any females she saw quickly looked away. Passing her paranoia off to the weed she'd smoked, she stuck close to Lucas.

Inside, the music blared. Heavy bass made recognizing the tune impossible. The farmhouse had been emptied of furniture and lit with black lights, and mounted colored Par Cans strobed in time with the music. Blackout curtains hung on all the windows, keeping the waning daylight out.

The air was thick with smoke, hazy and hot against her skin. Body odor, cigarette smoke, sweet vape juice, and pungent marijuana scented the air. Spilled alcohol mixed with dirt to form a foul skim of mud that tracked through every room and added its own tang to the miasma.

Lucas led Alicia upstairs.

The crowd parted in front of him and closed behind her. Anonymous hands brushed against her, there and gone before she could react. Alicia complained to Lucas, who acted like he couldn't hear her. At the top of the stairs, he pulled another joint out of his pants pocket.

Leaning close to her ear, he yelled over the music: "Here, hit this. It'll make you feel better."

She smoked this one alone after offering it to Lucas and the other guys standing in the shadows of the upstairs hall. All refused. Alicia's legs wobbled. She leaned against Lucas, and he supported her, then helped her into the bedroom at the end of the hall.

Inside, he dropped her on the only piece of furniture in the house: a bare mattress on the floor. Lit by a pair of battery-powered black lights, Lucas's teeth and T-shirt glowed purple. Blackout curtains hung along one wall. Alicia realized the entrance to the upstairs porch lay behind them when some of the guys came back inside. The group—it was hard to see how many there were—formed a circle around the mattress. Alicia jerked her head to Lucas, for the first time feeling seriously afraid despite the drugs clouding her mind.

"Boys, every season we win because we're the best," Lucas said. "We're the best because we work hard."

"Work!" the group shouted in response.

"Part of that work is becoming a team. In order to cement our bond as brothers, as warriors, we engage in the traditional rite of warriors of old. We bond in blood."

"Bond!" the group shouted.

Alicia tried to stand but couldn't get her feet underneath her. A hand pushed her roughly back down.

"Our tradition, our rite, our honor, our legacy begins like our warrior forefathers. Sacrifice."

Someone slapped her.

"Sacrifice!"

A fist smashed into her face. A foot buried itself in her stomach, knocking the wind from her body.

"Brothers, as your captain, your leader, your brother in battle, I offer this fresh fish. Victory in homecoming. Victory this season."

"Fresh fish! Fresh fish! Fresh fish!" Each exclamation was followed by two stomps.

Lucas dropped to his knees on the mattress and grabbed her sweater, jerking her toward him. The group continued to chant and stomp as Lucas took what he wanted. Then the others took from her too, scratching, biting, hitting, slapping, thrusting.

Alicia never even got the chance to scream. Why was he doing this? Didn't he love her?

While she was beaten and raped to the chant of "Fresh fish!" they laughed and drank. Dumping beer on her, throwing cans at her. The bass below thudded in time with the stomping. Alicia dipped in and out of consciousness.

After a time, she was alone with Lucas again. He carried her limp body, bloody and broken, back to his Mustang and dropped her in the trunk. Alicia lay in darkness, jolting painfully as the car made its way back to paved roads.

Sometime later—she couldn't say how long—the trunk opened again to harsh fluorescent lighting. Lucas carried her into tall grass and dumped her amongst garbage and dirt.

///

Tears ran down Mark's face. Her pain, her fear, her betrayal burned him. She'd suffered more than he had ever imagined. And her father had gotten a new car for his silence, for complicity.

Now we know what happens to them. We can help her, little brother. We can help them both.

"Then let's do it."

///

Alicia opened her eyes. Mark stood with his back to her, hand on the doorknob. She needed a minute to realize she was in Lexi's office, in her chair. Was Mark crying? Why was he crying? She felt drained, weak. Getting up from the chair wasn't possible.

"I'm sorry, Alicia. I'm so sorry."

"It's okay. I'm all right. What's going on?" she asked before falling asleep on Lexi's desk.

Mark opened the door into a nightmare.

///

Ciara sat waiting for Mark to return. He'd disappeared down the road close to half an hour ago. A man in a blue suit painted the fence along the road. She wasn't sure, but she thought he was talking to himself.

Then he stood perfectly erect, dropping the brush and can. Paint pooled over his shoes and onto the grass. He didn't seem to notice. Leaning forward, Ciara watched him turn a slow circle. The man took off at a run in the direction Mark had gone. No, not a run. A sprint. The guy bolted faster than anyone she'd ever seen toward the Colony grounds.

What was that about?

Ciara got out of the car, crossing over to Colony Road. Nothing suggested anything out of the ordinary. The air smelled of fall, wet with a promise of winter. Curious, she followed at a swift pace, hurried but not running. She'd wait for him in the lobby, and they could walk back together—assuming Mark wasn't in trouble. Trying to clear that thought away proved useless. The more she tried to dismiss it, the more certain she became that Mark was the reason for the guard's panicked flight back.

What else could it be?

At least she didn't hear sirens. She'd always associated trouble with the soundtrack of approaching sirens. Juvenile, she knew. Her pace quickened.

///

Wasps filled the hallway above Mark. Human-sized wasps. Thousands of horribly intelligent reflective black eyes turned toward him at once. Hundreds of sets of mandibles clicked, eager to rip and tear. The hallway reeked of ammonia. Upon closer inspection,

Mark saw they weren't exactly wasps but more of a human-insect hybrid. The extra set of legs were insectile, but fingers and toes were visible beneath stiff hairs that rustled and hissed with every movement.

Some flew, hovering above him. Most clung to the walls and ceiling. All faced him. Lexi stood watching him. "You come into my house, glamor me, glamor another queen."

"Lexi, I—"

"Be silent!"

The hive buzzed angrily at Lexi's tone. "I should let my sisters tear you apart. Not even you, Reptile, stand a chance here."

She speaks true, little brother. Much danger here.

Mark chose to remain silent, answering neither Lexi nor the reptile's obvious statement. Frozen to the spot, Mark wasn't sure what to do. Finding his way back through the confusing maze of corridors would be hard enough without a swarm of giant wasps.

"Twice you've disturbed the Colony. You've insulted me, undermined my authority, and violated the sanctity of our nest." Mark stepped out of her way and into the hall as she moved to check on Alicia. "If the new queen is hurt, you're dead where you stand. I will feed you screaming to the larva."

"I only wanted to help. I didn't mean to offend." Mark held his hands up.

A pair of antennae sprouted from Lexi's head as she leaned close to Alicia. The tips probed her sleeping face, rubbing her hair, exploring her ears, pushing into her mouth.

"She sleeps. At peace, unharmed." Lexi announced, straightening.

A hum echoed in the hallway, spreading out in all directions.

She has told the hive Alicia lives. She will let us leave, little brother.

"You wished to help only yourself. Imagining yourself a protector, an avenging angel, you came here to harness her pain, to arm yourself for your long-sought vengeance. Never mind if she asked for or even wanted it."

"I wish to prevent this from happening to anyone else," Mark said.

"You have brought her peace. This is the only reason you live. Take your revenge and never return."

Lexi led him out beneath the gaze of the hive.

Mark stepped outside and was nearly knocked over by Ciara hustling the other way.

"Mark! Are you okay?" she asked.

"He's fine. He was just leaving, Ms....?"

"Aleman. Ciara Aleman." Ciara held out her hand for Lexi to shake.

Lexi shook her hand and said to Mark, "I understand why. Still—" Her threat hung unsaid in the air between them.

"Yes, ma'am," Mark said.

Ciara watched the exchange, feeling the weight of something implied passing between them. Something she wasn't a part of. Hooking her arm in Mark's, she smiled at Lexi, then said, "Come on, handsome. Take me to dinner. I'm starving."

They walked arm in arm back up the road beneath the weight of Lexi's stare.

"Did you get what you needed?" Ciara asked.

"I did. Everything is going to be fine."

"Have you been crying?"

Ciara's mood was foul. All through dinner, she complained about going to the party with Lucas. Mark suggested she skip it, then spent the next half hour being berated for suggesting she had such a lack of character while her plate of lo mein grew cold. "You do what you say you're going to do, Mark. It's that simple."

"You clearly don't want to. I don't want you to. Blame me. I'll gladly be the bad guy."

"Sweet, but I'd still have reneged on my word. Integrity matters."

"I suppose, but I'm trying to give you a way out."

"I should never have agreed in the first place."

"I wouldn't do it. Lucas Gahan is bad news. I got Alicia to admit something bad happened and Lucas was responsible. She didn't say exactly what only that she ended up hurt. I don't want you getting hurt too. Even at the risk of sounding like a possessive, jealous boyfriend." Mark speared a bite of his General Tso's chicken. They'd agreed on a Chinese buffet style restaurant. Mark's paper place mat depicting the Chinese zodiac was stained with grease and sweet and sour from his attempts to eat his meal with chopsticks.

He wanted to appear worldly and sophisticated to impress Ciara, but after the third piece of chicken bounced into his lap, along with countless grains of fried rice, she wordlessly passed him a fork.

Taking the hint, he put the chopsticks down.

"He hurt her? How?"

"She wouldn't say." Mark inwardly flinched at yet another lie. "All she said was he'd hurt her and got away with it."

Ciara digested this latest bit of information. Her eyes lit up as an idea occurred to her.

"I'll go on the date. I bet I can get him to confess what happened. Then we take it to the cops."

"Ciara, no!" Mark's fork paused halfway to his face spilling more grains of rice, unnoticed, onto his lap. "We're not detectives and Lucas is dangerous. Like seriously. Besides anything he says to you would be hearsay. Please reconsider!"

Recognizing the stubborn set of her shoulders, Mark knew this was a losing battle. In his attempt to dissuade her he'd handed her motivation. Damn it.

"I was seriously considering breaking the date, but how can I now? I can get him off the streets where he'll never hurt anyone again. I'll record him on my phone. Hang him on his words. Besides, I promised my parents I'd go to make more friends. They're worried I'm spending too much time with a certain guy."

Mark decided to drop the conversation for now. He still had a little time to change her mind.

"Who is he? Sounds like a lucky guy."

"No one you know, and he is."

Ciara's mood worsened as the days moved closer to Friday. Her complaints sounded like she was displacing her fear to Mark. Pretending to be angry about one thing to hide the fact she was scared green. "Lucas said it's a special party for homecoming. What the fuck do I care about homecoming? Or football? Or meeting people who enjoy it? Ugh. Fuck my life."

Mark went to school, to work, and spent as much time with Ciara as possible. He said nothing about what happened at these special parties. It wasn't going to happen to her. He would make sure of that. Mark planned to be with her every step of the way.

Friday dawned cloudy and cold. The forecast predicted drizzling miserable rain all weekend. Perfect weather for Mark to follow unobserved. The cloud cover and rain would ensure little activity outside, and anyone looking up wouldn't see him.

After a quick sandwich for dinner, Mark ran up to his room. Ciara texted to say Lucas was on the way and to tell him she'd chosen a baggy hooded sweatshirt and jeans with a three-quarter length coat to wear tonight, hiding her body as well as she could. Mark decided to change as well.

///

Wayne glared at his useless tit of a son. "You're pathetic. Almost twenty-two years old and off to a high school party. You're a fucking embarrassment."

"Yes, sir," Lucas mumbled. He didn't mind. Nothing was going to spoil his mood tonight. Tonight, he'd be fishing. While she wasn't a freshman, tradition was still tradition. Age didn't matter. She could be a fresh fish, a sophomore slam, junior jam, senior slit, or college pussy—at the end of the day, she would be a sacrifice to the team all the same, to help bond them in battle.

"Don't think I don't know what you're doing. The same old shit you've done since high school. You're fishing tonight. Fucking sad."

"Yes, sir." Lucas imagined jamming his toothbrush into Wayne's eye. The surprised O of his mouth as blood and ocular fluid burst onto Lucas's hand. An erection pulsed against his jeans. Lucas leaned into the sink to increase the pressure on his groin. Wayne continued to humiliate him. Hard at the wrong angle, the increased pressure caused an involuntary shudder.

Tonight promised to be a good night. Not even Wayne could fuck that up for him.

///

Evening crept toward full dark as the shadow landed in the side yard between the Aleman household and their neighbors. The shadow curled around the trunk of a maple tree, vanishing among the upper branches. Anyone watching might have thought the wind combined with the low light played tricks on their eyes rather than an impossibility scrambling up the tree to disappear among the remaining autumn leaves.

No one saw.

The reptile kept his body close to the wet bark, altering his attention between the two houses on either side of him. In one, Ciara stomped around impatient, checking and rechecking her phone. In the other, a mother also stomped, calling for Ryan to come out of hiding and get in the tub right now. The reptile heard the boy shifting position in the upstairs bathtub.

She'll never find him in there.

A wash of headlights returned his focus. Lucas Gahan parked a lime-green Mercedes AMG behind Ciara's Accord. The reptile snarled, a soft growl rumbling in his throat. Lucas, dressed in a white T-shirt and jeans despite the cold drizzle, hustled up to the door. Ciara came out before he could knock. She spoke to him as she passed, making her way to the car. He leaned in for an awkward hug, which Ciara sidestepped, pivoting around and leaving him grasping empty air.

Good for you, girl.

Lucas shrugged and jogged back to the car. The engine growled to life, and the coupe's headlights illuminated the brickwork. Ducking low, the reptile wrapped his tail around the trunk and held perfectly still as the car backed up. He needn't have bothered. The evening mist thickened as the temperature dropped. Lucas would have barely been able to see the large maple growing between the houses, let alone anything lurking high in the shadow-filled branches.

After a quick check on Ryan's whereabouts—still hiding in the tub—the reptile took flight.

///

Lucas was getting angry. This bitch certainly wasn't making things easy. It'd be her tough fucking luck when they got to the party. She'd spurned every advance he'd made, flatly refusing any booze or weed. She kept her arms crossed and pulled away from him each time he reached for her. It was hard enough to get a look at her, buried as she was beneath the layers of her coat, sweatshirt, and attitude.

"Hey, I'm not out to ruin your day," Lucas said. "I want you to have a good time, is all."

"I met someone in the meantime, and I doubt he'd like you trying to get me liquored up."

"Maybe we can pick him up. If it'd make you feel better." Lucas had no intention of bringing her boyfriend. If she didn't want to relax, that was on her. Lucas intended on having fun with her anyway. Ethan and Lance had promised they'd make it. Lucas hadn't seen much of them since everyone went to college.

"I asked if he wanted to come with, but he had to work."

"Well, maybe we can go get him after he gets off," Lucas said before tuning out.

"Yeah, maybe." Ciara turned to face the window.

Lucas drove the rest of the way in silence, which worked fine for him. He didn't need her to talk, and in a few, she'd be making plenty of noise. Lucas shifted in his seat to increase the pressure on his erection and turned up the radio.

A shadow followed above, gliding underneath the base of the cloud cover. Moisture beaded along his body, rolling off claws, wings, and tail in fat droplets. Wispy tendrils of clouds parted in silent protest and closed fast in his wake.

Tracking the car wasn't difficult. His focus remained on the coupe. Traffic was light, and the blue-white bulbs of the headlights created a hazy bubble of light traveling through the mist. Thumping bass emanated from the car as it moved along the country road. Then another competing drone of music came from what must have been Lucas's destination.

The reptile circled. A farmhouse and barn shared a clearing bordered by thick woods. Many heartbeats beat beneath him. Cars parked haphazardly around the barn. Even from his circling height above the party, he smelled a foul miasma of smoke, alcohol, and pain. This was a bad place. Her bad place. She wasn't alone in her suffering. Many had bled here.

Foul intent stained the air as sure as blood stained the walls inside.

No glow escaped the house. The reptile knew the heavy curtains blocked the light. The place vibrated with pounding bass. Lucas was slow and careful in his approach, easing the Mercedes along. Even the earth seemed to want to keep people away from these tainted grounds.

Ciara was bored and ready to go home.

Her first foray into crime fighting was a dismal failure. She couldn't get him to talk about anything other than drugs, alcohol, or SVHS football. Lucas had disappeared into the house as soon as he'd parked the car. "When you're ready, come on upstairs. It's like the VIP section of the party. Downstairs will be mostly underclassmen, and I'm sure you aren't worried about making friends with them," he'd said. "I'm going to get a beer. See you inside."

Ciara had watched him go, not interested in the party but unable to leave.

She wondered what Mark was doing and wished he were with her. An odd feeling told her he was watching over her. Silly girl. Calling her father was an option, and she considered it. But how would she explain where this place was? Mark didn't have a car, and he was working anyway.

Why had she agreed to this? After meeting Mark, she'd regretted saying yes to Lucas, but her parents wanted her to meet other people and were worried about her getting caught up on a boy right away. They wished she'd go out and make some girlfriends. She had girlfriends in Charleston. Mark was here. And she'd never been with anyone like him.

A drunken kid—he looked like he was in junior high—staggered up to her. "I don't want to see you again without a beer," he slurred at her, forcing a can into her hand.

"Okay, kid." Ciara rolled her eyes and dropped the can as she walked away.

"Hey! That—that's a party foul!" he called.

Ciara raised her middle finger and kept walking.

"Damn! Fresh fish is spicy!" yelled a guy in a letterman jacket from the second floor. Like Lucas, he looked entirely too old to be at a high school party. *I hope when I go to college, I don't think of high school as the glory days like these losers,* Ciara thought to herself.

"I'm a senior, idiot. Not a freshman."

"Smell like fish to me."

Ciara rolled her eyes again and went inside. Unprepared for the cloud of smoke that rolled out as she opened the door, her eyes began watering immediately. *Great. Now I'm going to smell like weed when I get home.*

Equally jarring was the lighting inside. Par Cans placed around the house flashed, overtaking the black light. The air, humid with sweat and bad breath, clung to her clothes and hair. The place must have been abandoned. Graffiti covered the walls. An adage floated to mind about fools' names and fools' faces always appearing in public places.

The press of bodies made exploration difficult. Kids were everywhere. Some looked to be no older than thirteen or fourteen. Most were male, and all seemed drunk. One of the only girls Ciara had seen grabbed her wrist and yelled to her over the music. "Don't go upstairs."

Ciara turned to ask why, but the messenger was already lost in the cavorting shadows of the room.

She was beginning to sweat in her coat and sweatshirt—not that she was going to take them off. Several times, she felt curious fingers trying to sneak a feel, and the layers protected her to a degree. All she wanted to do was leave. For that to happen, she needed to find Lucas, which meant she had to disregard the girl's warning.

The stairs led to more shadows. While people were visible wandering the hallway upstairs, Ciara couldn't make out their faces. Like old ghosts, they haunted one room to another, cackling mad howls to the moon. Grabbing one person at random, she shouted in his ear, "Have you seen Lucas Gahan?"

He nodded, gesturing toward the end of the hall and saying something that was lost to the pounding music.

Let's get this over with. Ciara strode down the hall and opened the door.

///

He'd lost track of her. She'd gone inside. Continuing to circle, each loop lower, tighter, the reptile stretched out with his mind. He found a female, though not the girl he was searching for. Through her eyes, he saw

Ciara looking for someone. She appeared angry. Using the girl, the reptile approached Ciara and grasped her wrist. "Don't go upstairs," he warned, then was forced to release the girl.

While attempting to get this message to Ciara, he'd circled too low, almost flying into the side of the barn.

Fighting for altitude, he managed to pull himself above the roof line with a series of sprinting leaps. His claws ripped a path through the old metal. He angled around the house for another pass and found Ciara upstairs. Fighting.

Adjusting his angle, the reptile tucked his wings, rocketing toward the upstairs porch and roaring his fury.

///

After throwing open the door, Ciara crossed the threshold. "Lucas, I'm ready to go. Now."

This room was different from the others in one respect—it contained a dirty mattress as the sole piece of occupying furniture. The guy who'd said she smelled like fish shut the door and stepped in front of it, leaving Ciara trapped, surrounded.

The low light made it difficult to recognize faces, though Lucas she knew because he stepped away from the group of silhouettes surrounding her. "Okay, fish. I tried to make this easy for you. Remember you wanted it this way," he said.

Not waiting to see what the plan was, Ciara turned and kicked fish boy in the balls. He doubled over, holding his wounded scrotum, the smirk gone from his face. She stepped forward and stomped the instep of the guy next to him before bringing her forearm into his chin. The force of the blow knocked him through the rotted plaster wall and into the hallway.

Seeming surprised by the ferocity of her attack—apparently "fish" weren't supposed to act like this—the group stepped away as she jerked the door open. Lucas wrapped his hand in her hair and jerked her back into the room. Fighting for balance, Ciara twisted into him, slamming her fist into his ribs with all her bodyweight behind her. Lucas took the blow, grunted, and punched her once, twice, then again in the stomach.

She dropped onto the mattress at his feet, the wind knocked from her. The group in the room recovered from their initial shock and descended on her. Ciara tried to ball up and protect herself from the flurry of punches and kicks. Someone stomped on her chest as Lucas struggled with her jeans. Her position and the rain of blows from the jostling males made it difficult for him to get a hold of her.

A roar unlike anything she'd ever heard filled the room, drowning out even the deafening music. The assault paused as her attackers looked around the room at each other. The glass doors to the porch exploded into shards. Bits of wood shrapnel and broken glass peppered the occupants in the room.

Those with their back to doors were flung forward as something entered the room. It roared again. Ciara put her head down, screaming, and then the weight on top of her was gone. When the room was silent, still, she opened her eyes. Her attackers lay everywhere. Their blood covered the floor and splattered the walls, and Lucas was gone.

The reptile burst through the doors, knocking boys to the ground. He turned, lashing out with fang, tail, and claw to clear an exit path. The reptile jerked Lucas from where he crouched on top of Ciara, then leapt back into the night. Pumping his wings, he carried Lucas higher and higher. What he intended required concentration. He couldn't allow himself to crash into a tree or a barn.

Lucas wiggled in his grip. "Let me go! What are you? Dear God, let me go!"

In the misty cold air far above the ground, the reptile invaded Lucas Gahan's mind. The filthy cesspool of rage and degenerate urges was almost enough to make the reptile drop Lucas and let him tumble to the earth, where the ground would absorb his deviance as it absorbed his life blood.

But he held on even tighter instead. A small grunt of satisfaction escaped his throat as he heard Lucas's shoulder break.

Lucas shrieked. "You're hurting me! Why won't you let me go?"

Because we have somewhere to go together. A date.

The monster spoke into his mind! Its eyes glowed blue-white like the headlights of the coupe. Falling into that awful light, where his secrets were laid bare, Lucas burned with humiliation. This thing knew everything he'd ever done. Closing his eyes to block out the images of what he'd done, what he was, and the shame of it all did no good. It was in his head, forcing him to see.

He was the fish from three years ago. The reptile forced the memories onto him. In Lucas's mind, he was both criminal and victim, beating and raping himself. Alicia's pain became Lucas's, and Lucas became his own victim. His friends, brothers, raping and beating him. Shame. Burning, humiliating shame.

Yes, the thing in his mind whispered. *Yes, feel her, become her, become what you did. Experience it! Embrace it! It's yours! Now, forever, yours.*

"No. No. No. No. It's not fair. It's not fair. Why?" Lucas howled to no one.

His sanity snapped. Mind broken, he thrashed to be free of the demon holding him. Somehow, he jerked himself loose, and then he was falling. Thankfully falling, until the images stopped, replaced by merciful darkness.

The reptile watched as Lucas fell onto the radio tower of the defunct WBAD station. Metal burst through his chest, pinning him 450 meters above the ground. Diving in for a closer look, the reptile saw Lucas had died with a smile on his face, rain now filling his open eyes.

"How the fuck did that happen? Did someone throw him out of a helicopter?" Inspector Walsh of the Commonwealth of Virginia Bureau of Investigation wondered aloud. If this wasn't the strangest crime scene he'd worked, it was in his top five. How do you impale someone fifteen hundred feet up?

Friends and neighbors, if that wasn't enough, the victim was forcibly taken from a party at an abandoned house four miles away. The place was torn all to hell and the location of a possible sexual assault led by the guy currently dangling on an antenna, and no one was capable of saying who or what had snatched him.

According to the trail of physical evidence, Walsh's current theory was King Kong the Impaler had prevented an attack on his girlfriend by tossing the perp onto a radio tower and vanishing back to Skull Island. Sure. Made as much sense as anything else.

"We have anything yet on flights in the area?" Walsh asked. Grasping at straws, but he had to check. Professional, thorough, Walsh dotted all his I's and crossed all T's, even when it was a wasted effort. He knew a loser when he saw one, and this case was pure grade A stink.

A helicopter crew hovered above, attempting to bring the body to earth. Engine roar and rotor wash inhibited conversation. Walsh wasn't thrilled with a helicopter hovering over the crime scene, but what could he do? The body couldn't remain atop the tower until it decayed.

A uniform—name tag read Smith—brought him a copy of registered flights from Summit Airport. Any flights in the area would have had to register their flight path and tail number. The log was federally mandated—one thing the federal government got right, in Walsh's opinion, though he held no hope of a flight crossing over last night.

Sometimes unexplainable things happened in Summit Valley.

At the farmhouse, things were equally dead—pun intended—crowded with drunken high school kids and even a few middle schoolers out of their minds on alcohol, marijuana, Molly, and whatever the fuck else didn't make star witnesses. Most were so scared of the cops they didn't speak at all.

Those at the epicenter of the chaos were particularly tight-lipped, with one exception. Ciara Aleman. Walsh scheduled an interview with her later in the afternoon. A cursory debriefing with the uniform who'd talked to her on scene made Walsh admire her. Kid was a fighter.

She claimed an attempted rape by four seniors, three underclassmen, and two Summit Valley High football alumni. Claimed she'd almost fought her way free when Lucas Gahan, her date, stopped her escape. Lucas, only child of Wayne Gahan, one of the largest employers in Summit County, had been kicked out of school for raping an unconscious girl behind a dumpster.

A history of rape. How about that?

Walsh knew as sure as he stood there that Daddy had paid massive amounts of money to keep Junior out of jail. Laws for thee but not for me. The helicopter crew, having cut the antenna below the body, lowered the corpse. The remaining antenna jutted from the chest cavity like an accusatory finger. Walsh watched impassively as the body was released from the carrier.

With some relief to those working the ground, the helicopter crew left the scene. Silence descended in its wake. The investigative unit gathered in a rough semicircle around the body.

"Never saw anything like it," an EMT Walsh didn't recognize said.

No one responded.

Lucas Gahan was covered in cuts. Small chunks of glass and wood stuck out of his face and body. His left arm and shoulder had a sunken, malformed look. Walsh bet they'd find Kong the Impaler had crushed the kid's shoulder before flinging him up on the tower, and he'd bet his pension the glass and wood matched the busted glass doors at the farmhouse. Worst of all was the awful grin frozen on Lucas Gahan's face. *Mortuary is going to have a hell of a time fixing that face,* Walsh thought. *Closed casket for sure.*

It seemed having a defunct antenna rip through his chest was preferable to whatever had come before. Walsh shuddered. "Well, he's dead. Bag him up and take him to the coroner for autopsy. I doubt we'll learn anything. I can feel my clearance rate bursting into flames and leaping off a fucking cliff."

///

Lucas was bagged and loaded into the back of an ambulance. The EMT wrapped the body, careful to preserve the state of it for the coroner, who'd remove the antenna in a controlled setting. Lucas took his final ride to Summit Valley Community Hospital wrapped in black plastic—a grisly pup tent—insane joy forever frozen on his rigor mortised countenance.

The EMT, Nathanial "Nate" O'Barr, rolled the tent from the ambulance to the morgue. His sister-in-law,

Michelle, worked for Gahan Motors in a managerial role. O'Barr left the body, stepping outside for a cigarette and a quick phone call.

Word spread quickly. Wayne Gahan knew his son had been murdered before any police showed up to inform him. He made his way to the hospital and demanded to see the body within thirty minutes of O'Barr's phone call with his shocked sister-in-law. According to Michelle, "It couldn't have happened to a nicer guy."

///

Einar waited until midnight. Shady dealings were best conducted under cover of darkness. The hospital never closed—not really—but the graveyard shift at a small-town morgue was often deserted late at night. A lone attendant and a security guard trying to date her were all that stood between Einar and his prize.

Mark performed beautifully.

Dropping Lucas on the radio mast seemed a bit dramatic to Einar, but reptiles did what they wanted. Strolling into the morgue unmolested, Einar scented the air: chemicals, disinfectant, vomit, meat, excrement, and blood overtop underlying death. Sweet, sweet perfume.

Harsh fluorescents overhead permitted no shadow. Painted cinder block, a sick industrial green, contrasted with the white counters and cabinetry lining the walls. In the middle of the orange-brown tile was an unoccupied steel table—a shining altar to the dead. It dominated the space, drawing the eye. Einar paused to admire the sleek drains, the table's shining utilitarian function.

"Hey! You aren't allowed in here."

Einar turned toward the voice. The security guard, hand on hip, glared at him.

"In that case, I'll be quick." Einar grabbed the guard by the shirt and threw him into the wall. The back of the guard's head burst like overripe fruit, spraying blood, brain, and skull in a crimson fan. The body slid to the ground, leaving a scarlet snail's trail on the cinder block.

"Festive," Einar remarked, admiring the contrast of red and green. "At least cleanup will be a breeze."

He turned his attention from the cooling corpse to the double row refrigeration units housing the less recently deceased residents. Of the ten metal doors—stainless steel like the autopsy table—three were occupied: an elderly heart attack victim; an unfortunate drunk who'd fallen from a railroad trestle, snapping his neck on the creek rock; and one Lucas Gahan. Einar opened the door labeled Gahan, L and extended the table. It rolled smoothly, fully extending and clicking into place with a satisfying thud. Einar unzipped the body bag.

"Beautiful, beautiful. Aren't you perfect?"

Lucas's face, still contorted in its ghastly smile, stared unblinking at the overhead lights. With the metal removed, a horrendous wound in Lucas's chest exposed broken ribs, missing organs, and the black plastic beneath him.

A bit of brain fell from the ceiling behind Einar and landed with a wet plop.

"Yes. Yes, you'll do fine. Just fine."

Book III

Lucas fell over and over, grinning at Mark in his dreams. Mark woke with a start, the nightmare shocking him awake. Strange—he felt nothing about Lucas's death. Lucas had been a vile rapist, and he'd gotten what he deserved. Mark felt empty. Taking life, human life—even subhuman like Lucas—should have meant something. Mark wasn't upset with what he'd done.

He called Ciara under the guise of wanting to know how her date went.

Mr. Aleman answered her phone. "Hey, Mark. Ciara isn't up to any calls right now. She's had a rough night and only went to bed an hour ago."

"Is she okay?" Mark asked.

"She will be. Look, I probably shouldn't be the one to tell you this, but I'm her father, so I will. Lucas Gahan attacked Ciara last night. She says he tried to rape her. They were interrupted, and Lucas was found impaled on a radio tower a few miles from the party they went to. No one seems to know how it happened." Mr. Aleman paused. "And I really don't care."

"Oh my God," Mark said, injecting surprise into his voice while he pictured Lucas's face, smiling as he fell. "I'll be right over."

"No, Mark. Give her some time. She'll call you when she feels up to seeing anyone. Until then, give her some space. Be patient. She's been through a lot."

"Yeah—I mean, yes, Mr. Aleman. If there's anything I can do, anything you guys need, please call. Seriously, Mom'll cook dinner, or we can bring you something. Whatever she needs."

"I appreciate that, Mark, and Ciara will too. Thanks for checking on her. You're a good boy. We'll talk to you later."

Mark hung up, wondering if he should go over anyway. Mr. Aleman had no idea what Ciara had gone through last night. Mark did. He'd been there with her, protecting her. Maybe he'd fly over tonight and check on her. Make sure they hadn't hurt her.

Lucas had been on top of her, struggling with her pants when Mark burst through the door. A crowd had gathered, watching, waiting their turn.

Mark dropped his phone into his jeans pocket. He needed to get to work; he'd promised Millie. After work, he'd run by Sonic and pick up a vanilla Dr. Pepper for Ciara.

///

Wayne Gahan's face contorted in an ugly snarl. High color bloomed in his unshaven cheeks, which were otherwise drained of color. Pale, shaking with rage, Wayne fought to control himself. Michelle had told him Lucas was dead. That bitch didn't care Lucas had died. She'd worn this sarcastic little smirk on her face when she relayed the news.

After rushing to the hospital, he'd found they wouldn't let him see the body or even acknowledge Lucas was there.

Nobody would talk to him.

With the threat of a lawsuit called in from his attorney, Wayne was led by a harried administrator to the office of the chief operating officer of Summit Valley Community Hospital, Benedict Warner, a full day after he'd arrived at the hospital. Mr. Warner gave Wayne a cup of coffee.

Hands folded together on his desk, Mr. Warner leaned forward, announcing Lucas's unfortunate death in a sober baritone. "I'm sorry as hell to be the one telling you, Wayne. You've always been a generous supporter of this hospital, and we care about you—about Lucas—a great deal. Our thoughts and prayers go out to you in these trying times."

Wayne quivered with outrage. Their thoughts and prayers? Fuck their prayers. Lucas was his heir. The last piece of Julia. His legacy. A generous supporter of the hospital? Wayne wanted to slam Benedict Warner's head into his $20,000 glass top desk, make him bleed some of that blue blood onto the Persian carpet.

What the fuck did Benedict Warner know about anything? Had he started from the gutter? Built an empire with his bare hands? Lucas had been a tit, but he was still Wayne's son. Had this silver spoon-sucking moron in front of him ever lost a child? After losing a wife? How could a man who kept a rug like that know suffering?

"Please, Mr. Gahan, take all the time you need."

"Where is my boy?" Wayne asked through clenched teeth.

"You're upset. I can only imagine. I'm a father as well. I feel just awful about what you've been through. Rest assured, I'll investigate how you were treated earlier myself and make sure it never happens again."

"Where. Is. My. Boy?"

"Mr. Gahan, there was an incident in the morgue last night. We lost a security guard."

"What does that mean to me?"

"Mr. Gahan, I'm not sure how to say this... Whoever killed the guard, well, also took your son's body."

Wayne stared at Mr. Warner, with his expensive silk suit and razor cut hair, soft hands folded demurely on his desk, then threw his cup of coffee in his pseudo-concerned face. The mug shattered as blistering hot coffee went everywhere. Wayne jumped out of his seat, looking remarkably like Lucas two days prior, and punched Benedict Warner once, twice, three times in the face before slamming his head into his desk. A fine web of spider cracks spread out in all directions, obscuring the global map underneath.

Wayne turned, pausing to roll up the Persian carpet, and left the office with the carpet under his arm, feeling better than he had in two days.

///

Inspector Walsh sat in the Alemans' living room two weeks after the party. The more he spoke with Ciara, the greater his admiration grew. She was tough, damn tough, and had nearly fought her way free. Her boyfriend sat beside her, arm draped protectively around her shoulders. Ciara didn't need protection.

A girl like that might take the law into her own hands.

Walsh didn't want to jump to any conclusions, but facts were, in the two weeks since her attack, six of the ten attackers had been murdered. On his lap, he held a list of the names of the boys who'd been in the room with Ciara on the night of Lucas Gahan's death. The seniors—varsity players all—Jacob Finck, Tyrone Lorhner, Noah Patrick, and Jason Ramirez had been treated for minor cuts and bruises after the incident and released to the custody of their parents. Of the four, Finck, Lorhner, and Ramirez were dead, along with their families. Beaten into pulp, torn to pieces. Crime scene photos were some of the worst he'd ever witnessed.

The underclassmen who'd been in the room, Gregory Murray, Trey Lorhner—brother of Tyrone—and Brandon Avery, had also been released to their parents after treatment for minor injuries. Brandon Avery had an older brother, Lance, who'd been invited to the party but was unable to make it. Lance used to run with Lucas when they were in school together. Brandon remained free, bebopping along without a care.

Tyrone had been at home with his brother and parents when whatever blender broke loose. The Murray boy had been found with his head mashed into the front lawn. The rest of him had remained untouched, but the head was crushed with tremendous force. So much force, in fact, that the head—or the remains of the head—lay at the center of an impact crater.

Ethan Gilmore, another one of Gahan's running buddies, was back at the University of Virginia shit scared and nursing a black eye. Ciara had knocked him through the wall in her escape attempt. Walsh hadn't brought formal charges against Gilmore yet, but they were coming.

Fourteen murders, counting the family members caught in their sons' webs, in a two-week span. Summit Valley was awash in blood. The only connections were the football program at the high school and the girl sitting cuddled up with her overly protective boyfriend. Neither looked capable of such carnage, but Walsh made no assumptions.

Anywhere else, this kind of carnage made national news. But not here. Not this place. Summit Valley kept its own secrets. Every time his police radio chirped, Walsh cringed, positive it was another body. Or group of bodies.

"Are you aware most of your attackers are dead? Six out of ten, more than half. In two weeks. Along with their families?" Walsh tried a little shock and awe.

The girl reacted as expected.

"I'd say I'm sorry to hear it, but I'm not. They were going to gang-rape me. Saying it out loud feels surreal."

"You don't find it odd? Suspicious, even?"

"I'm sorry at the loss of life, even degenerate lives, but I can't say I feel bad. Karma is a nasty bitch sometimes."

Her mother balked, holding a hand to her chest. "Ciara! Language!"

Walsh was shooting in the dark, and he knew it. The boyfriend, Mark Branton, was at work or home when the incidents took place, and Ciara had remained under her parents' watchful eyes. He'd already confirmed their whereabouts before this interview. Like most of this case, it was turning into a formality.

Summit Valley kept its secrets.

"I'm sorry, Mother, but I hope the devil is shoving flaming pineapples up their asses right now."

"I can't say I blame you." Walsh stood. There wasn't a killer in this room. He was just crossing the T's and dotting the I's.

Ciara sat at the computer in her room. Open on her monitor was the free version of an audio editor program. She stared at the wavelength on screen. The program allowed her to drop the background noise, in this case a booming stereo. She'd left her phone recording in her pocket throughout her date. Most of the audio was useless.

Lucas bragging in the car, inviting her upstairs, snatches of drunken conversations.

"We're taking state again this year."

"Machinegun Kelly is fucking fire."

"My nuts itch. Think that's normal?"

And her friend who didn't want to see her without a beer.

She'd skimmed the waveform until she heard a faint, "-anted it this way."

Hand shaking, she highlighted the next thirty seconds of audio. Cropping that into a new file she began to play with the filters. She managed to drop the music almost completely out. Engrossed in figuring out the program she pushed the sound of her struggles to the back of her mind. Memories ached sharp as fresh bruises.

Rewind.

"-you wanted it this way." More tweaking of the various sliders and knobs on screen. The overpowering bass beat faded while voices and noises grew more pronounced.

Rewind.

"-you wanted it this way." Sounds of struggle. Ciara lost in phantom punches almost missed it.

Rewind.

"-you wanted it this way." A screech. A roar, faint but distinct. Growing louder. Growing closer.

Rewind.

"-you wanted it this way." No doubt about it. She stared at the small peak on the waveform where the creature who took Lucas announced itself. After the fight began. After they attacked. It had been watching, waiting. It knew something was going to happen.

It knew.

Mark lay in bed thinking about the inspector's words. Those boys were dead, murdered. Did he have anything to do with it? Could he have possibly, as the reptile, done something so heinous?

Wasn't us, little brother.

Mark wanted to believe. He always remembered his exploits when he returned to human form. There weren't any blackouts, no memory loss. Only an inexplainable sadness at releasing the reptile when it came time to change back. He loved the power, the strength. The reptile was savage, yes, but it was directed savagery.

Einar had seemed to relish in the hunt. Mark thought about him crushing pigs in the sounder or dropping out of the air to crush a deer head into the dirt. Einar was happiest, most himself, on a hunt. Could he have been enacting revenge on Mark's behalf? Doing what Mark wouldn't?

It didn't fit. Something was happening. The party had set a chain of events into motion, and Mark felt strapped on a train speeding to an unknown destination. Off a cliff? Into a wall? Somewhere worse?

He needed answers.

He needed Einar.

Though Einar hadn't been around lately. Not at Coopers Cave or the surrounding wood. Mark couldn't find him anywhere. It seemed Einar had decided he wasn't going to be found and vanished. Smoke in a high wind.

Deceiver, the reptile whispered. *Trickster*.

Wayne Gahan stood alone in his empty living room, feeling like the last pea rattling around at the bottom of the can. Curling his toes on his new rug and sipping a twenty-one-year-old Hibiki brandy purchased after Lucas's birth, he watched the New River flow on its ancient bed. At $900 a bottle, the brandy burned smooth and subtle. Julia was dead, buried years ago now. Lucas too. Except there wasn't a body for Wayne to bury this time. Someone had broken into the hospital, killed a guard, and stolen his son's body.

Wayne had never pretended to possess an overabundance of affection for the boy. Once he'd reached puberty, Wayne recognized him. His own father had enjoyed beating and raping women. And little boys.

Chiefly his own. When Wayne met Julia, she'd given him the courage to act, to break free of the old man.

With Julia, he'd been able to bury a knife in the old bastard's ribs.

That night, they'd celebrated with champagne on a ridge overlooking the New River. Lucas was conceived that night. Later, Wayne bought the property and built their home there, overlooking the New River, where he and Julia had had their first real taste of freedom. After that, the sky was the limit.

When she gave birth to Lucas, Wayne tried not to see his father's eyes staring at him out of his son's face. The boy grew to look more like him, and he inherited more than looks from the grandfather he never knew. Lucas had Wayne's father's cruelty, his viciousness. Julia recognized it too, though she pretended not to.

She somehow knew her time was limited. She made Wayne promise to protect the boy. Lucas was her song—she called him that sometimes—and she wanted Wayne to protect her song. After she'd gone to her maker in a brutal car crash, Wayne did his best to honor her. He raised Lucas and fought the desire to drown him and let the New have him, even when he knew what Lucas was.

Not that any of it mattered now. Lucas was dead. He'd failed.

Wayne rested his forehead against the glass, blessedly cool. The New River ran its course, indifferent to his heartache and reflecting house lights just as it had since he'd first seen it with Julia, though a few more houses dotted the ridgeline now, and the trees were a little thinner.

A heavy knock on the door startled him. He spilled the drink he'd been nursing over the course of the evening. "Damn it!" Wayne searched for a towel, a rag, anything to dry his hand, then settled for the back of a couch cushion. Whoever was at the door better have a good goddamn reason for disturbing him.

Three more slow knocks rattled the door in the frame. Wayne had enough alcohol in him to know he should've been afraid but also enough not to care. He removed a .45 Sig Sauer 1911 from its hiding place underneath the hall table and walked over to the door. When he paused to peek through the peephole, the heavy pistol fell from nerveless fingers, clattering to the floor.

Wayne backed away from the impossibility banging on his door.

Again, three heavy knocks. Wayne doubted the steel core door could protect him from the monstrosity for long. His feet slid out from beneath him as he stepped on the .45, and Wayne sat down hard. His teeth clicked together, and he bit his tongue. Coppery blood filled his mouth, making him gag.

Boom.

The door groaned.

Boom.

Cracks formed around the frame. Plaster dust fell like a fine brief snow.

Boom.

The framework collapsed. The steel core door, still shut and locked, fell inward along with the frame that had held it in place. Windows shattered as the glass impacted marble tiles, peppering Wayne with a fine grit. Wayne scooted backward, unable to look away from the thing on the other side of the gaping hole.

"Knock, knock, Daddy," the thing said, ducking its head to step through the threshold. Its rumbling voice reminded Wayne of planned avalanches he'd witnessed vacationing with Julia—tons of snow falling, grinding, and churning the earth before it. The creature stood over eight feet tall. The granite gray of its flesh absorbed the light. A darker gray circle on the chest, rough as though filled with gravel instead of flesh, caught Wayne's eye. The inspector had said Lucas was impaled through the chest on a radio tower.

Lucas's eyes stared at him.

This thing was his son, somehow impossibly alive. Joy, swift and savage, fought the paralyzing fear Wayne felt. The Gahan bloodline lived! "How are you here? They told me you were dead."

Stepping forward to embrace him, Lucas said, "Laws for thee, Daddy. Not for me."

///

The reptile flew above the New River, searching for the Gahan property. Wayne Gahan might've been responsible for the recent streak of violence in Summit Valley. Everyone knew Wayne had been a common thug before meeting his wife. She'd turned him from small-time criminal to something worse. She made him legitimate. Helped him achieve recognition, fame, money.

Thanks to her, Wayne gained the ability to throw money at his problems until they went away. Mark suspected that without her and Lucas, he'd reverted to his old ways. Without someone to control and direct him, maybe he was enacting a revenge fantasy against those who'd failed to protect his son. Was the theory thin? As tissue paper. But Wayne Gahan was the last person Mark could think of who might be capable of this kind of violence.

Aside from Einar, who he couldn't contact.

Mark was sure the Gahan estate overlooked the New River. From the air, he could see both sides of the river and the houses that bordered it—those by the bank and those farther up the ridgelines. The Gahans' estate had to be on the ridgeline. They wouldn't be content having someone looking down on their home. Wayne liked to pretend he was king of Summit Valley.

The river flashed by beneath him. His dark wings blended perfectly with the night sky. The silver on his stomach reflected the house lights on the river's surface like flickering starlight. A few cars traveled the roads paralleling the New River. Lonely headlights cut the darkness, unaware of what traveled the night alongside them. Skeletal branches strained to catch him as he passed.

A cold wind blew this close to the water, carrying the scent of the river: wet earth, decay, dead fish.

A crash ahead drew his attention.

The palatial home overlooking the river dominated the ridgeline. When seen from the air, the home resembled the letter C, with a curve of polarized glass facing the river. Large, gaudy, and completely incompatible with the surrounding countryside, this had to be the place.

The reptile alighted on the roof above the front door—or where the front door used to be—silent as a dream. Blood. The smell of it was strong. Leaning forward to curl his long neck down, the reptile inspected the hole. From his upside-down vantage, he saw the hallway was filled with blood and bits of meat. Einar stood in the hall, dipping his fingers in the pooled blood and then writing on the wall.

The reptile dropped down from the roof. Einar? What are you doing?

Einar's reaction was immediate violence. He pounced forward and grabbed the reptile behind the head before he could withdraw, his stony hands cutting off his air, then swung him into the wall, crushing drywall to powder and splintering framework. Maintaining his grip on the reptile's neck, Einar swung him again, this time overhead, into the marble tile of the hallway.

Dust burned the reptile's eyes. He needed air. Motes danced in his vision. In desperation, he lashed out, raking his claws across Einar's chest. With an incoherent roar, Einar swung him a third time and launched him through the house. The reptile shattered through the glass wall, tumbling back outside. Sweet air flooded back into his lungs. Trees scratched at him as he fell end over end until finally landing in the river. His body ached from the beating he'd taken. The reptile spread his wings, attempting to fly, but pain shot through him. Managing to crawl to the bank, the reptile felt gratitude for the numbing cold and the soft mud before the world went dark.

///

Mark awoke, naked and shivering, as dawn lit the eastern sky. Everything hurt. He needed to move, but he was so cold he couldn't think. How far from home was he? The reptile had withdrawn deep within him.

I hurt, little brother.

"Me too," Mark whispered through chattering teeth before passing back out.

///

Voices. Arguing. About him? Yes. And pain. So much pain.

"He looks like he's been choked. Did you look at his throat?"

"Yes, I saw his throat; I helped you carry him in! Poor thing looks like someone tried to kill him."

"We need to take him to the hospital."

"We should call the police."

"No. We can't have police here. Can't we just drop him off at the ER?"

"This isn't a movie. You can't drop someone off and drive away without a million cameras recording you."

"What if whoever dumped him comes back?"

"It looked like he crawled out of the river."

"Our luck."

"Okay. He seems stable for now. Let's just wait for him to wake up."

Mark was no longer naked. He'd been cleaned off, and someone—the owner of one of the voices, he assumed—had clothed him in sweatpants and a T-shirt. He lay on a bed in an unfamiliar room. Mark groaned as he sat up. Outside the window was the bank he'd crawled to the night before. The Gahan estate sat on the ridgeline above. Mark could also make out the path he'd taken when he crashed through the trees.

He was warm, but his throat hurt, and he was hungry. With little option on what to do next, Mark decided to seek out the people who'd rescued him. And hopefully something to eat.

Inspector Walsh arrived at the Gahan estate at seven that morning. He'd been up for hours. He typically didn't sleep much, and a part of him had expected a call. The drive out was uneventful, but as soon he parked, he spotted a uniform puking into the bushes.

Another man—Walsh assumed the groundskeeper who'd called it in—stood looking away from the sick cop. Dressed in dirt-stained jeans and a faded red T-shirt, with two days' stubble on his face, the man had the deeply tanned and lined skin of a someone who worked outside. The whites of his eyes, yellowed from years of smoking, shone with intelligence. Leaving the uniform to finish his business, the man approached as Walsh stepped out of the car.

"You call this in?" Walsh asked.

"I did."

"Inspector Walsh."

"Randall Miller. Folks call me Randy." They shook hands. Randy's were the calloused, rough hands of a working man. With nicotine stains on his fingers and wild hair poking out from underneath a faded San Antonio Spurs 1999 NBA Champions hat, Randy gave the impression of a man who saw much and said little.

"What happened?"

"Can't rightly say."

"Tell me what you can."

"Showed up around five thirty—"

"This morning?" Walsh asked.

"Eehlup."

Walsh nodded. "Continue, please."

"Pulled up. That's my truck over there." Randy indicated an aging Chevy. "And noticed the big damn hole in the wall. Looked inside. Didn't go in. Called you guys. He"—he nodded toward the sick policeman—"showed up, went inside, ran back out to yarp in the bushes. Then you got here."

"You work for Mr. Gahan?"

"Eehlup. Near four years. Cut grass, trim bushes, plant flowers."

More police in marked cars rolled up the driveway. Walsh motioned for one to get Randy's information for further questioning. "Also, get this virgin out to direct traffic," he said, and the sick officer left to stand by the road and manage the scant traffic.

The house stank like spoiled meat. Blood soaked everything—the walls, the ceiling. It had even pooled in the cracks in the tile. Signs of a struggle—a knock-down, drag-out—were evident in the hallway. The picture glass in the living room had a giant hole in it. Something had gone through there with incredible force. Those panes were rated to withstand hurricane force winds.

The front door had been knocked completely out of the wall.

On the walls, written in blood over and over, hundreds of times, a manic pronouncement of insanity read Laws for thee. Not for me.

"What the fuck is happening around here?" Walsh wondered aloud.

///

Mark sat eating breakfast with Tom Day and his wife, Emma, elderly retirees who supplemented their income growing and selling marijuana. Tom worked as a music teacher at Radford University, and Emma was a career journalist. Neither retirement paid for much, but their clandestine farming allowed them to exist quite comfortably. Tom sold in bulk to former students, who grossly marked it up and sold it to current students. Tom also kept a small distillery, which Emma used to make apple pie moonshine.

"I can understand why you didn't call the police." Mark took a bite of Emma's homemade blueberry waffles. He moaned. "These are so good."

"Slow down, honey. No one is going to take them away from you," Emma said.

"What kind of night were you having to end up naked on my bank?" Tom asked. "Bacon?"

"Yes, please. You wouldn't believe it," Mark said around a mouthful of waffle. "I was fishing..."

Easy, little brother. Say little.

"A bit cold for that," Tom said.

"Better to catch big catfish when it's cold. So, anyway, I was fishing and guess I nodded off. My pole was jerked out of my hands. It means a lot to me because it belonged to my dad, so I dove in after it."

"Why were you naked, dear?" Emma asked.

"I didn't want to get my clothes wet, so I stripped down. When I jumped, I hit a log or branch or something. Stabbed me right in the throat. Knocked the breath out of me. I sucked in a big mouthful of river water, got disoriented, and hit my head on the boat, which I guess has floated away since the anchor wasn't down. I managed to make it to shore, where you guys found me."

Not little, little brother.

"Boy, I've heard some whoppers, but that one's a champ. I bet you were partying with friends, dropped acid, and howled at the moon all night." Tom grinned.

"Honey, if he doesn't want to tell us he had a bad trip, he doesn't have to. But, Mark, we've all been there."

"Sure have," Tom agreed. "Hell, if you'd knocked on the door, Emma or I could have guided you down. No need to sleep in the cold. You don't want frostbite on your bits, son."

Mark's cheeks flushed. "I'm sorry. You're right. I was partying with friends and ran off through the woods chasing chickens."

"Why were you naked?" Tom asked.

"I don't know."

Yes, little brother, simple is best. Let them believe the worst.

"Was that so hard?" Emma asked.

"I guess not. It's just embarrassing."

"No need to be embarrassed." Tom clapped him on the shoulder. "Like Em said, we've all been there. Bet you got beat all to hell running naked through the woods."

After breakfast, Mark called Ciara, who insisted on picking him up. He handed the phone to Tom, and he explained to her how to find them. Half an hour later, she was knocking on the door. Still in the sweatpants and T-shirt Tom had lent him, Mark opened the door. Ciara smiled at him and stepped in to meet his rescuers.

"Boy had a bit of a wild night, so go easy on him," Tom said.

"Wild night?" Ciara raised her eyebrows.

"Long story," Mark said, burning to leave. Ciara was going to ask questions he had no answers for. She knew he didn't do drugs. She'd want to know why she had to come to a stranger's house to get him. She'd want to know why he was found naked. Hard questions without answers. She eyed his bruised throat when she thought he wasn't watching.

"Not really," Emma said. "Honesty is the foundation all relationships are built upon. She came to get you. Be honest with her."

"Can we have this conversation later?" Mark asked.

Studying his face, she finally nodded. "Fine."

"Thanks for everything." Mark tugged on his clothes. "I'll bring these back."

"You're going to be all right, young man," Tom said as they headed for the car.

After waving goodbye, Mark's rescuers went back inside.

///

Ciara drove in silence for a few minutes before pulling over. Removing her cell phone she played the enhanced audio. Mark heard the roar as Ciara was attacked.

"It was you," she said.

"What was me?" Mark asked, knowing where this was going but helpless to stop it.

"At the party. You. How?"

The reptile roared warnings for him to lie, to stop talking, to mesmerize her. But he couldn't do it. Looking her in the face and uttering a blatant untruth wasn't something he felt capable of. Not to her. Ciara deserved better.

Against the ferocious warnings in his head, Mark answered, "Yes."

Afraid to say anything else, he raised a hand, quivering with nervousness. He willed a silver claw to push free. He extended it a few inches, ignoring the drops of blood that ran down his finger and forearm to drip from his elbow onto Tom Day's sweatpants. Then the claw withdrew into the tip of his finger, leaving the skin smooth and unblemished. Only the blood trail down his arm remained. Irrefutable crimson proof.

Ciara watched the demonstration with widening eyes. Mark expected her to kick him out and run away. Instead, she took his hand and kissed the tip, getting a smudge of blood on her lip. "Does it hurt to do that?"

"More than you know. Do the cops have a copy of that?"

"No. It felt wrong to give it to them. I don't know why; I didn't want them to have it. What are you, Mark? You're not dangerous—not to me. I know that. But what happened to you?"

Mark released a breath. "I'm a kid who went camping because I missed my dad. I wanted to feel close to him again. While I was there, I met a man who gave me something that"—he struggled to describe what had happened to him—"changed me."

"What was it?"

"A spirit of sorts. We're bonded. He speaks to me, calls me little brother. Right now, he's furious I've told you this much. Together, we become greater than our parts. Because of the reptile, I was able to follow and protect you that night. I'd never hurt you. I knew Lucas raped and beat Alicia. The reptile saw it in her mind. Together we took the memory from her and used it to protect you."

"Somehow, I knew it. When I was in that room, with them all around me, I knew if I fought long enough, you'd show up. I never doubted it." Ciara took Mark's hand, holding it with both of hers. Her skin was soft, warm. "Mark, I need to know if you're killing people for me."

"I'm not, Ciara. I swear it. Even Lucas got away from me and fell. I went to Lucas's house last night searching for some clue as to who is doing this. Anyway, when I got there, I saw my mentor."

"The guy who changed you?" Ciara prompted.

"Yes. Name's Einar. He can change too, but not like me. He resembles a gargoyle—tall, scary, stony skin. He was in Lucas's house and beat me half to death when I approached him. Threw me in the river."

"And you managed to get to shore and changed back, hence naked guy on the lawn."

Mark smiled. "You got it, kiddo."

"Why would your mentor attack you?"

"I'll have to find him to find out."

"He must fear you, then. Fear what you'll grow into."

An aging Bonneville cruised by at a sedate twenty-five miles an hour. It was the only car they'd seen. A late season sparrow landed on the hood for a moment before flitting away. The New River rolled along like it always had. The morning, overcast and cold, announced winter wasn't on the way; it was banging on the door, demanding entry.

Mark shook his head. "Einar isn't afraid of me. He's playing a game I know nothing about." He paused. "Though I guess I'm not even sure that was him last night. Just because I haven't seen another gargoyle doesn't mean others aren't out there."

"Okay, if it isn't Einar, then who is it? Why are they killing the ones responsible for attacking me? If they're doing that, am I in danger? Are my parents in danger?"

Mark didn't know. She had so many questions he didn't have the answers for. Every time he got involved, things went wrong. His investigation had gone completely sideways. The more Mark thought about it, the more he believed the thing that had attacked him wasn't Einar. But could it have killed Einar? Is that why Mark hadn't seen him lately?

Ciara was waiting for him to answer.

"Ciara, I don't know. I'm so out of my element. Every choice I've made has been wrong. I fucked up with Alicia, nearly screwed up protecting you, and my half-assed detective work got me thrown out a window and nearly drowned. I don't know what to do."

She squeezed his hand. "You saved me. Whatever else happened, without you, I'd have been another victim of Lucas Gahan. Raped and forgotten. You stopped it from happening, Mark Branton. You. I'm sorry Lucas died, but I can't help feeling he brought it on himself. I'm not losing any sleep over him, and you shouldn't either. I don't know what happened with Alicia, but I doubt she blames you for what happened, no matter how badly you want to take it on yourself. The best we can do is..."

Be calm. Be still.

"...continue to be there for each other. We'll stay close to each other, see how this shakes out."

"The reptile agrees with you. He says we need to be calm."

"That's because I'm right." The corner of her mouth lifted in a half grin. "So far, this other gargoyle is attacking rapists."

"And their families. Don't forget them."

"Yeah." Ciara sighed. "What we can do—really, all we can do—is keep an eye out. And if it comes back, you'll stop it."

Her faith in him made him uncomfortable. "Because I've done such a bang-up job so far."

She leaned over to give him a small kiss. "You've got motivation now."

Mark grimaced. "You still have blood on your lip."

※

Mark's mom was at work, and a note on the counter told him she'd left a sausage biscuit in the fridge for him. The biscuit disappeared in four large bites, chased with milk from the carton. Mark went upstairs, changed out of Tom Day's clothes, and took a shower. His body ached all over. He'd never been much of a fighter, and another round with Einar—if it was even Einar—had made him feel ill. He'd been thoroughly trounced.

After calling Millie to beg off work—again—Mark wanted rest. His bruises were fading even though they were only a few hours old. A good sleep in his own bed would help even more. Bone followed him, curling up at his feet. Mark was asleep seconds after his head hit the pillow.

///

The rest turned out to be exactly what Mark needed. He woke feeling refreshed. Positive, even. Bone watched him bound out of bed, then laid his head back down with a sigh. Mark grinned at the big dog, who apparently wasn't done with his nap.

Upon waking, an idea occurred to him. If Mark watched one of the others who'd been involved in the attack on Ciara, he might be able to intercept Einar or some other shape-shifting gargoyle—he couldn't find it in him to believe Einar responsible—before he killed again. Knowing next to nothing about their habits, life cycles, temperaments, or any other relevant details beyond what Einar had told him about their kind, Mark was flying blind.

Mark had a plan of sorts and pulled out his phone to run it by Ciara. It felt good having someone to talk to. For a long time, Mark had felt so isolated and alone without anyone to give him advice. The simple act of confessing to Ciara unburdened him in a way he hadn't thought possible. Even better, she hadn't run screaming or kicked him out. Instead, she'd listened with patience and understanding. More, she still liked him!

Ciara thought his plan was sound. Mark politely turned down her offer to help, preferring she stay far away from this craziness. Three possible targets remained and only one Mark. Thirty-three percent chance to get it right. Not terrible odds, but not fantastic either.

Ethan had gone back to college. Mark recalled that he'd been accepted to UVA to play for the Cavaliers. Mark had no intention of flying to Charlottesville to watch Mr. Gilmore hit on coeds. Assuming he could even find Ethan. UVA was a big school. Mark wasn't close to Ethan, didn't like the guy, and had no idea where he lived.

That left Brandon Avery, the underclassman, or Noah Patrick, the senior.

A stakeout on either one might lead to his quarry. Or his quarry might kill him this time. He picked Noah Patrick because the Patrick family lived farther back Caseknife Road and deeper in the mountains than he did, meaning hiding and watching wouldn't prove difficult. Mark would know if anything was coming before it got to the house.

The farther back one traveled on Caseknife, the fewer homes there were—farther apart, separated by thick woods, with less chance for someone innocent to be caught in the middle. He'd been lucky at the Gahan place. He'd underestimated the reaction of the creature, and it had stomped him.

Mark didn't intend to give it another chance. The most successful predators were ambush predators.

One major drawback was the farther back one traveled on Caseknife, the more the likelihood of getting shot by a paranoid landowner increased. His father used to tell of a time when even the police didn't ride into the hills on Caseknife Road uninvited. Mark never worried; Caseknife was home. He walked the road into town and back every day, though never venturing farther than his own home.

It was a rule everyone followed, but now seemed as good a time as any to violate that rule.

The Patricks lived on a steep hillside near where Caseknife became Ridge Road. Deep in the woods, surrounded by nature, the Patrick homestead crouched on the side of a mountain far back from the roadway. It was the kind of home you wouldn't notice unless you were looking for it. No one came looking for the Patrick family without invitation.

Rumors floated around town that the Patricks had taken up making methamphetamine after the fire destroyed their still. Noah Patrick was the oldest of six children who ran the gamut, from ages four to eighteen. Noah was big. Noah was mean. A solid lineman for the Summit Valley High School Demons, he was on his way to Virginia Tech on a full football scholarship once he graduated.

If he didn't end up in jail first.

Noah was pure brute—mean tempered, tough, the product of generations of poor hopelessness. No problem existed that he couldn't solve with his fists. He paid little attention to Mark, interested in younger, weaker, slower prey. Mark moved a bit too fast and had filled in too much for Noah to consider him a target. Mark still avoided Noah as a rule.

Reaching out, Mark felt for the minds inside the house. Noah was home, playing video games while his father slept in an upstairs bedroom. The rest of the family was...out? Shopping? Yes. Out shopping. Mark scanned the grounds to find a place to hide and watch.

Standing on the ridgeline above the Patrick house like he'd been waiting for him was Einar. Motioning for Mark to join him, Einar sat with his back against a towering black oak tree—one of many near the top of the ridgeline, where the wind scoured the branches, leaving a crunchy padding of dead leaves below. Skirting the edge of the property, Mark left the road to sit beside Einar.

"Heard you made a friend last night," Einar said.

"I thought it was you."

"No, dear boy. I'd never. Notice his chest?"

"The darker gravely bit? I might have seen it as he threw me through the window."

"Your handiwork, my boy. As well as his current state of mind. That's also your fault."

"My fault? How so?" Mark asked as the conversation took on an accusatory tone. Einar never acted this way toward him. He seemed angry, offended.

"You broke his mind. He's completely insane. He made a perfect gargoyle—and may still—but he'll never be human again. Not such a bad thing, really, but he'll need to learn to hide. And I'm afraid hiding isn't his nature."

"What are you saying, Einar?"

"I've already said it, Lord Reptile." Mark didn't miss the venom Einar spit at him. "I came to Summit Valley for him but found you and thought you might have potential despite your proclivity for canines. In my defense, I'd never dealt with a reptile before."

"You aren't making sense." Mark's head whirled. Einar hadn't come to Summit Valley because of the Song? He was searching not for Mark, but for someone else?

"Now he's trapped in an endless loop, believing he's being attacked. If he destroys his attackers, maybe he can break free. That's my hope, anyway."

"But you said the stones led you. The Song."

"I've told you the barest minimum. When it became apparent you weren't the right sort, I began searching for another. I found him in a morgue. Human body destroyed, mind shattered. My protégé—my real protégé. A pure gargoyle. We'll be breed again without the stones. Just like the wasps do."

"You're telling me that thing is Lucas?"

"Yes, dear boy. And here he comes now."

A high-pitched whistle grew in intensity as Lucas dove out of the sky. Tucking his wings, increasing his already tremendous speed, Lucas hit the roof of the Patrick home. A living bomb, twisting and corkscrewing, he used his weight and incredible momentum to rip through the house, taking the supporting structure with him.

Driving a growing cloud of shrapnel before him, Lucas passed through the bed where Mr. Patrick slept oblivious. One minute, Mr. Patrick was having a dream about his wife's sisters—getting a good boner in the process—and the next, he ceased to exist. Noah had enough time to register something might be wrong before the living meteorite pounded him into the basement as fine mist.

The effect on the house was immediate and devastating.

A groan came from the farmhouse walls as they buckled and broke, then fell into the basement. The remains of the roof collapsed inward with a crash and a cloud of dust. Glass tinkled as shards burst out of window frames twisted to proportions never intended. The rubble shifted and groaned again before coming to rest.

Mark jumped to his feet when Lucas crashed through the roof, and Einar disappeared, leaving behind only his laugh, which blended with the death groans of the house. The earth rumbled as the middle of the sloping yard bulged upward.

A stone hand burst free, showering the area with dirt and gravel. Another hand tore its way loose, flinging more debris skyward. The hands came down, and flat palms pushed the hidden body out of the ground. With a roar and a tearing of constricting earth, Lucas emerged from beneath the grass as if the land had aborted an abominable fetus.

Dirt and remnants of the house, plaster, and blood mottled stone skin. A scrap of wallpaper clung to his massive thigh. Splinters of wood stuck up behind pointed ears—a crown of destruction. Mud streaked his chest. His eyes, shining red, glowed with hate and insanity. Open bulldog jaws pulled in great heaving gulps of air. He craned his head back, extending his wings, and roared again, celebrating his devastating triumph.

Willing the change to come, Mark ran down the hill.

Too tired, little brother. We can't.

"Give me something!" Mark yelled as he leapt at the creature's back.

His claws burst from his fingertips in time for him to bury them between the thing's wings. The roar this time was one of agony as Lucas thrashed. Mark held on until a heavy wing batted him into the hill he'd just run down, knocking the breath from his lungs.

Before he could sit up, Mark found himself pinned beneath a large stone foot. Lucas leaned in, his tremendous weight grinding Mark into the dirt. When he brought his face in close to study him, Mark gagged at the rotten meat smell on its breath. He growled, a low rumble deep in his throat. "I remember you. Squash you."

Mark ceased his vain struggle to remove the foot from his chest. Instead, he rammed his claws into the spaces between Lucas's toes. He howled, leaping backward. The sudden push away drove Mark deeper into the hillside. Hopping on one foot, Lucas leapt skyward, blood raining down like a biblical plague. Mark pushed up on his elbows, watching Lucas fly away. Then the world spun, and he blacked out.

///

Mark's eyes cracked open an unknown amount of time later. He was still in the hole, and a cold turbulent sky churned above him. Three late season sparrows sat on his chest, cocking their brown heads at him. Mark groaned and sat up. The sparrows fluttered into the yard a few feet away, still watching him.

"Yeah, I know," Mark said to the birds. "I got my ass kicked again. I was stupid to charge him."

The birds seemed to nod in agreement with his assessment.

"I got excited, all right?" Mark felt foolish speaking to birds, but the reptile didn't answer.

Painfully, he got to his feet. The birds flew up to watch him from the safety of the trees. Mark hobbled past the ruins of the house, now silent and settled. He didn't feel any life inside the rubble.

Mark shuffled to the road, his stride becoming easier and more natural the farther he walked. Time to go home, take another shower, and put on yet another change of clothes.

Brandon Avery was the last one alive from the party.

Aside from Ciara.

///

Twice now, he'd come up against the creature —Lucas Gahan but not—and twice, he'd been pounded into the dirt. This time literally. The sparrows followed him home, treetop to treetop. Their company comforted him.

At home, Mark changed clothes and dumped his dirty outfit in the washing machine. Gargoyle blood stank. He washed himself in the shower, finding several small cuts previously unnoticed on the back of his head. Clearing the drain of the small rocks and larger bits, he lingered until the water ran clean. Mark toweled himself off, then gingerly patted his wounded skull. In his head, a plan to stop Lucas's rampage began to form.

///

Ciara parked behind her father's truck. Mark had saved her. He'd crashed through the glass door and protected her from the horror within. While worried about her, knowing she was in danger, he hadn't fought her decision. Instead, he'd followed from above, her personal guardian angel, watching, waiting.

Some girls might've been mad about his lack of faith, but Ciara knew it wasn't her Mark didn't trust. It was him—Lucas. She'd meant what she said to him; in her eyes he was a hero, not a monster. A monster wouldn't have followed her through the storm. A monster didn't care if another terrorized the people.

Mark had used his...abilities to help. She didn't know how else to think of it. Something had blessed him, magnified the goodness in his heart, the sweetness in his soul. He thought himself a failure. Believed he'd failed her like he'd failed Alicia. Ciara didn't see it that way.

"You like your car so much you're gonna sit in it all day?" her dad called from the door.

Ciara blushed, then got out and walked over to him.

He put his arm around her. "Come on in. We have cookies!"

///

For three days, Mark, Ciara, or both made rounds past the Avery household. Set in an older but well-maintained section of Summit Valley, the Averys lived in a brick ranch that sat back from the road. This section of town near the epicenter had been hit particularly hard by the fire and was one of the first to spring back from the destruction.

The old trees were gone, consumed along with the old homes, but the fire cleared out the brambles, leaving the ground nourished and fertile. Grass sprang up, and the squirrels returned to stash caches of seeds. Soon, young trees pushed their way out of the ground, easily moved to more desirable locations. New families, new life, rebuilt over the ashes.

The Averys were one such family.

Land was cheap, the town desperate to repopulate, and incentives to build in Summit Valley lured the Averys in from North Carolina. John Avery, a contractor, recognized the opportunity to move his wife and son into a larger home for less than what they paid in rent in Raleigh. Plus, they'd own their home.

Convincing his wife, Cecilia, wasn't difficult; she was sick of the traffic and crime associated with city life and was quick to agree. With enough work to go around rebuilding the town, John brought his sought-after skills to Summit County and was soon one of the top contractors in the area with enough offers that he had to turn many away.

Brandon Avery, on the other hand, wasn't on board with the move. He'd spent much of his short life in a gang founded with two friends. They called themselves the Knights and were petty criminals accelerating toward some serious trouble. Starting with minor theft from gas stations—candy or pornographic magazines—they graduated to extortion and marijuana sales by the seventh grade, which Brandon repeated twice.

Brandon loved hurting people, loved the power he had over them. At nearly six feet by the eighth grade and weighing close to two hundred pounds, he reveled in bringing pain to someone weaker than himself.

The move to Summit Valley removed Brandon from the Knights, ending his budding criminal career. Lucas Gahan recognized Brandon's potential immediately and took the freshman under his wing. Brandon quickly learned the joys of being an Inner Circle member of the football team and maintaining a high enough grade point average to remain on the team became paramount in his life. The Averys credited Brandon's remarkable turnaround to athletics.

The Inner Circle gave Brandon access to the fresh fish parties. He could beat on people—on and off the field—and be celebrated for it. It was way better than being a Knight. When hanging out with Lucas or Trey or Greg, he found himself among kindred spirits. They didn't care if he was slow. The IC only cared about him being big and being mean. He'd fought his parents on the relocation but soon felt Summit Valley was the greatest thing that had ever happened to him.

Until Lucas Gahan died after the last fish party.

Brandon didn't even get a piece before something blasted through the door, peppering him with glass and splinters before slapping him aside. He didn't think it possible for someone to hit him as hard as he'd been hit. When he staggered to his feet, Lucas was gone and the IC were lying on the ground. The fish ran out and blabbed to the police.

Then, one by one, the members of the IC began to die.

Brandon was smart enough to recognize the pattern, and he was the last of the guys left from the party. Something was hunting them—killing them—and he didn't know who to go to for help. The police weren't an option. Neither were his parents, for obvious reasons. Both were suspicious as to what had been happening when Lucas was abducted. The fish had made his life all kinds of difficult.

He'd seen her cruising by his house the last couple of days. Sometimes she was alone. Other times, she was with some nobody he recognized from school but didn't know the name of. Brandon thought about going out to talk to her. Perhaps she finally wanted to give him his turn. Then he'd think about the former IC members and change his mind. Inside was better. Safer. There were other concerns besides the stalker fish and her stupid boyfriend.

Like, who would host the next fish party?

///

Ciara circled the roundabout, driving back by Brandon's house. She'd seen him watching through the curtains and knew she'd been spotted, but it didn't concern her. Mark was with her, and last time Brandon had crossed Mark's path, things didn't end well for him. Even without, Mark she wasn't afraid. Brandon was strong, sure, but he was slow. Stupid. Too stupid to realize they were trying to protect him.

Plus, Ciara figured the years studying Krav Maga with her father gave her a serious one-on-one advantage. She'd put one of those big idiots through a wall before Lucas grabbed her. No, Brandon Avery didn't scare her a bit. But the thing hunting him did. That thing—Mark said it was a crazed Lucas Gahan made of stone—kicked Mark's ass every time, even when Mark became the reptile. Doubtful Krav Maga would be much help in that case.

"Looks clear," she said to Mark.

"Yeah. Nothing going on. I don't feel anything nearby either. No Einar and more important, no Lucas."

"What do you want to do?" Ciara asked.

"Head home. I'll check later tonight."

"Stop by the house first?"

"As long as your folks are cool with it."

"I'm sure it'll be fine. Hey, you can talk to me." She tapped her temple. "Right?"

Mark shrugged. "I don't know. I've never tried."

"Try."

"While you're behind the wheel? No way." He shook his head.

"Go ahead, chicken."

"*Nix, nein, fräulien* . Ain't happening."

"Bok, bok, b-gok!" Ciara teased, flapping a faux chicken wing.

You are so beautiful. I'm falling in love with you.

Ciara stomped the brakes, and the car behind her laid on the horn. As the driver passed, he gave her the finger, but her attention was on Mark. "I heard you," she whispered, eyes filling with tears. "I think I'm falling in love with you too."

"Ciara?"

"Yes?"

"Can we get out of the middle of the road?"

///

With the coming night, the change would be upon him. It was getting easier. Mark stood naked by the window waiting for the sun to set, his senses becoming hypersensitive. His mother snored softly in front of the television downstairs, two floors beneath him. Bone also slept unaware. Outside, a skunk investigated the pen where the trash cans were kept. That one he both heard *and* smelled.

The sun sank a little lower—barely a fiery sliver behind the evergreens now, burning its hydrogen into the void, sinking lower and a little lower still. The moon, rising low and dirty in a sky the color of a deep bruise, would be full tonight. He stretched. The change was closer with the coming dark.

Soon, little brother.

He opened the door leading to a rooftop deck and remained just inside his room. Better to do it now. The sun finally dipped below the mountains. Raising his arms to the sunless sky, he embraced the change. The tingling began in his neck and ran down his back, like blue flame down his spine. His body prickled and burned as nerves shifted and realigned. His neck extended; his facial bones broke and reformed. He fell to the floor and crawled toward the outside air.

His fingers and toes extended, gaining an extra knuckle each, and shining silver claws burst from the tips with little dribbles of crimson. His spine elongated, freeing his tail. With a groan that was more a reptilian hiss, black leathery wings burst from his back. New muscles grew, stretching to accommodate the new appendages.

Why had he thought this was getting easier?

Crawling on all fours, mindful not to scratch up the floor, he made his way out to the deck. Realizing something is wrong Bone is now scratching outside the door, whining, wanting to help. Mother snores on, unaware. Relishing the newfound power in his limbs and the feel of cool night air on his scales, he filled his lungs with it and extended his wings. Then he leapt off the deck.

It was time to hunt.

Mark promised to stop by Ciara's house this evening and he intended to keep his promise. First, though, he decided to make a quick check on the Avery's on his own. Beneath him, Caseknife Road snaked its way through the mountains toward Summit Valley. Streetlights twinkled like exotic gems on black velvet. The new clock tower on the courthouse was close to completion but jutted toward the sky, black as necrotic flesh. The town itself was lit in anticipation of the coming gloom and made the courthouse seem even darker in comparison.

Angling northeast, he passed over the Avery household before continuing to Ciara's. Feeling a slight pang of guilt for not heading directly to her, the reptile stretched out his mind, feeling for the life beneath. Nothing amiss, nothing panicked, only the night beasts waking to do their rounds and the Averys gathered in their living room watching a sitcom. He pumped his wings, gaining altitude.

The streets were almost empty. Summit Valley went to bed early. Only the occasional lonely headlights illuminated the darkened streets. The reptile glided high above, unseen, riding invisible air currents toward Ciara.

A hollow bong drew his attention. Then a flapping motion beneath him. It came from the rebuilt clock tower. Something leapt from the tower, struggling to rise on the light currents over town.

Lucas crawled from his lair in the clock tower. The images in his head assaulted him—thrusting, punching, biting, bleeding. The dreams—always there, awake or not, haunting him. Holding his hands to the sides of his head, Lucas smashed his forehead into the wall once, twice, and again. The images continued to attack, laughing at his pain, his blood, violations by him, violations of him, confusion, hate, rage. Laughing, constant laughing. His pain was a joke to them. To who? He wasn't sure. He would kill them all, tear their flesh. Kill who? Them. All of them. Everyone.

Recreated to encourage tourism, the upper workings of the clock tower included an English full-circle ringing bronze bell. Clappers wrapped in thick padded leather to muffle the chime lent a mournful sound when the hour struck. Moonlight filtered through the glass clockfaces mounted in the walls, highlighting the dust in the air. Scaffolding covered both interior and exterior walls, providing support and a workspace for the lapidists and masons involved in the ambitious project. Doors installed into the clockfaces provided access for custodial or maintenance purposes. Lucas used these doors as an entrance to the tower's heart.

Winter's approach slowed construction, and Lucas was left undisturbed in the space to dream his awful dreams. He couldn't remember who he was, exactly, or what had happened to him, but something horrible had entered his life in shards and splinters, much like his thoughts.

He remembered darkness and cold, then a feeling of complete peace being snatched from him with the coming of light. Lucas hated the light for bringing pain and confusion, longing for a return to calm darkness. There were no voices laughing at him there. No terrible pain from his back to his chest.

Roaring, Lucas slammed his head into the bronze bell. The boom echoed in the hollow tower. Ringing decibel pressure drowned out the laughter for a moment—one pain purging another, however briefly. With the purge came temporary clarity.

Lucas. His name was Lucas.

His father hated him.

Something had attacked him. He'd fought it and won. No longer human, he'd become greater, stronger, faster. He had wings! Laws no longer mattered. He'd been given a gift of impunity, immortality. Nothing could hurt him again. No one could stop him. Lucas Gahan was a law of nature, a law unto himself, free.

"Laws are for thee, not for me. Not for me. Not for me. Not for me. Laws for thee, not for me." His father used to say that to him—before Lucas crushed him to pulp. "Not for me." Once he'd finished with the ones who'd hurt him, Lucas would be released from their haunting voices. Two left.

Lucas smashed through the maintenance door and stepped into cool starlight. The moon greeted him as an old friend. Spreading his wings, Lucas jumped and pumped furiously to gain altitude. From above, a shadow aligned itself to his flight path.

///

Ciara sat between her parents watching television, though it was mostly on for noise more than anyone's general interest, and they kept the volume low. They discussed nothing of importance and merely enjoyed each other's company. It was Ciara's favorite part of the day. Correction: her favorite part of the day without Mark.

This family ritual went back to her childhood. As far back as she could remember, their family had spent the last two hours before bed relaxing together. Ciara reclined on the sofa with her feet in her father's lap. Her mother, Michelle, sat in her recliner, which was angled to share an end table with the couch. Trent Aleman sat on the far side of the couch so he had a good view of both his girls while he rubbed his daughter's feet.

On the television, large men in flannel shirts and suspenders competed in the Lumberjack Games. Trent liked watching the guys try to roll each other into the water during the log roll event. Michelle, absorbed in a book, contributed when the conversation caught her attention. She secretly liked the burly men with their shirts clinging to thick chests and shoulders, but she'd never admit it. Ciara found it incredible people were paid to throw axes and chop wood.

Fidgety and unable to relax, Ciara sat up, tucking her feet beneath her. Anxiety ran up and down her spine like a kitten on a keyboard. She had no logical reason to be afraid, but her blood pounded in her temples, unspent adrenaline causing her thighs to shake. Getting up from the couch, she went to look out the window.

Grove Street was quiet. The families in her neighborhood kept early hours. Suburban domestic rituals were being conducted in the brick homes lining both sides of the street. Dinner dishes were being washed, children bathed, television watched, teeth brushed, and jammies donned. Absolutely nothing out the ordinary.

But her anxiety escalated, screaming at her to run.

"Honey, you feeling okay?" her dad asked.

"I'm fine, Dad. Thought I heard something outside."

"What is it?" her mother asked.

"Nothing. I'm freaking out a little, I guess." How could she explain she wanted them to get in the car and leave? Right now. Before it was too late. Why, she couldn't say, but Ciara found herself unable to deny the feeling of impending doom.

Ciara! Run! Get out! Coming in hot! All of us!

Lucas had been hiding in the clock tower. Of course. Where else would a gargoyle hide?

The reptile angled to intercept him but changed his mind before closing the gap. Pulling up to gain altitude on Lucas, he slowed to match his speed. Lucas might've been powerful, but he had zero grace. Instead of angling himself to rise, he flapped manically, trying to use brute force to make his way into and through the air.

The reptile followed at a distance. At this height, he didn't think Lucas would see him should paranoia strike. At his side, a group of sparrows glided along, four to his left and three above his right wing, coasting on the displacement. The birds weren't known for night flying unless disturbed.

Lucas wasn't heading to Brandon Avery's house. The Averys lived behind them to the west. That left only one place he could be going: Ciara's.

Tucking his wings, the reptile accelerated, intending to crash into Lucas from above and drive him into the earth. Wind rushed by, howling in his ears before sliding across his scales like oil.

I can't let you do that, Mark.

Ciara did the only thing she could think of—she screamed. "Oh my God! Dad! Someone's stealing my car!" She ran to the front door and flung it open, feeling satisfaction that her parents followed close behind.

"Hey!" Trent yelled. "Get the hell out—"

The house collapsed inward where the Alemans had just been watching the lumberjacks compete. A warm push of air filled with stinging grit and splinters knocked Ciara toward the street. She rolled down the yard before coming to rest in a tangle of limbs. Both her parents landed close by.

Struggling to stand, Ciara was knocked over again as an inhuman scream filled with rage, hate, and pain obscured even the sound of her collapsing house. The windows exploded from her Accord and her father's truck, peppering them with glass. Car alarms went off down the street, adding to the cacophony.

Hoping that wasn't Mark, Ciara picked herself off the ground again.

///

As the reptile impacted Lucas, Einar crashed into him. The three tumbled in an uncontrolled ball of gnashing teeth and slashing claws. The reptile dug its rear claws into Lucas's back, burrowing them deep. With his front claws and teeth, he savaged Einar's chest and shoulders. All three tumbled uncontrolled toward the earth.

///

Lucas struggled to free himself from whatever was digging into his back, but his attacker's angle made it impossible for him to reach. Wings flailing uselessly, he thrashed his arms, managing to catch a stony ankle. Yanking with all his strength, he threw the attacker toward the swiftly rising ground. The attacker—another like him—crashed through the roof of the home below.

Einar might have blasted into Mark with devastating force if the reptile hadn't rammed Lucas first. Instead of delivering the blow to the reptile, Einar instead felt Lucas's wing crumple between them, popping and cracking as bones shattered within their stony casing.

The reptile grabbed Einar by the upper arms, repositioning him so his face and chest were vulnerable as the rapidly approaching ground switched places with the stars and back again. It might have killed him, so fierce was the attack, but Lucas gripped his ankle, crushing it before flinging him into a house. Einar impacted the foundation with terrible velocity. Concrete, wood, and plaster exploded outward as if he were a meteor fallen from the heavens.

Before Einar could gather his senses Lucas landed on him crushing him deeper into the impact crater. Structural integrity compromised beyond the breaking point, the Aleman's home collapsed into the impact site. More debris fell on Einar's head. In the darkness, Lucas bellowed his insane roar, deafening in the confines of the collapsed house. A heavy foot kicked Einar in the head over and over as Lucas scrabbled to free himself from the rubble. Once, twice, again, and then Einar knew only darkness.

///

The reptile rode Lucas into the hole in the roof. Then, using Lucas as a springboard, the reptile bounded nimbly back out, simultaneously driving Lucas hard into the ground. Leaping free of the collapsing home, the reptile gained enough altitude to remain hidden among the rising dust and darkness. Beneath him, Lucas battered his way out of the twisted mass.

///

I'm fine, Ciara. Leading him away. Are you all right?

"We're fine. Minor cuts and scrapes is all," Ciara said out loud.

"Yeah, we're fine. Thanks to you," her father said.

"Baby, how did you know?" asked Michelle.

"I didn't know anything. I thought someone was breaking into my car."

Jiggling the door handle, Trent said, "Locked up tight. Whoever it was can have the damn car. Did us a huge favor."

Drawn by the noise, neighbors came out to inspect the damage. The windows of the vehicles on either side of the Aleman home were now shattered and glittering on the ground. Otherwise, the neighborhood remained undamaged.

Trent looked on as the dust rose. "What the fuck happened to our house?"

///

Lucas's wing ached and hung at an odd angle. Worse, his back on either side of the spine leaked a foul-smelling fluid. Movement was difficult. The dragon-like creature flew off to the northwest. Unable to fly, Lucas followed on foot. Rage drove him on. It had attacked him. Laughed at him. Now he would catch it, tear its flesh, gnaw its bones.

Gripping his wounded wing, Lucas yanked hard to straighten the appendage. Intense, blinding pain made him stumble. He'd never catch it staggering along on the ground. He had to fly despite the pain. An inner voice directed him to focus his will on mending the wing. Lucas didn't argue.

Kneeling in the grass, Lucas imagined it whole, undamaged. He focused harder. His wing began to burn, then itch. Shattered bones within knitted together, driven by Lucas's stony resolve. Torn muscles found each other. His cracked armor reformed, and the pits and gashes in the wing healed. After testing the limb, Lucas decided it wasn't quite whole again, but he'd healed it enough to continue his pursuit.

Stumbling slightly, his back still bloody, Lucas took to the air. Grasping with his hands as if he could pull himself skyward, kicking his feet, Lucas broke gravity's hold with his physics-defying awkward flight. The voice in his head helped quiet the other voices and directed him toward his attacker. The filthy ambusher continued to the northwest.

Run all you want, Lucas thought. *It won't do you any good. I'm coming for you.*

The reptile felt the mad beast healing himself. Even at this distance, the force of Lucas's will was unmistakable. A malevolent tide rushed its way toward the reptile, intent on carrying him into seas of madness. He had to stay in front of it. The element of surprise was gone. His sneak attack had been ruined by Einar. The reptile knew he'd never defeat anything that far within the depths of insanity.

Strangely, he felt at peace. Alive. A darkness worse than anything he'd ever known pursued him, and yet he felt like laughing. The stars caressed him. Moonlight wrapped him in warmth. Beneath him, night creatures went about their rounds, life continuing despite the dark.

Streetlights mirrored the stars above. He felt the serenity of the void filling him, bestowing the primal unfathomable power of the infinite. Evil pursued relentlessly behind, but it didn't matter. The night opened to him, offering all her possibilities.

REPTILE

The reptile slowed his pace, circling, allowing the beast to remain close. Best not to get too far ahead. The thing was simple, best to let it believe it could catch him. Circling again, he heard the babble of Lucas's broken mind drawing closer—eager, confident, positive it would soon have him.

Moving on, the reptile led the thing farther into the countryside.

///

Lucas felt the dragon-like creature ahead of him. Running. It was scared and slowing down. Getting tired.

Good.

Pushing harder, willing more speed from his fragile wing, Lucas charged ahead. His prize, his tormentor, lay beyond the ridgeline. Climbing higher, he sought to escape among the sparse cloud cover. Too much moonlight lit the sky, and billion stars betrayed the ambusher, the tormentor, the enemy. Thick ropy strands of saliva leaked from his jaws at the thought of vengeance. Lucas's retribution would be fearsome.

When the sun rose, it would shine into the tormentor's gutted body cavity Lucas would leave for carrion.

A flash split the night.

An explosion ripped along the ground, throwing earth and fire into the sky. Thick smoke followed. Lucas found himself unable to see. Struggling to hover in place, he was pulled inexorably downward. A stinging pain in his neck caused him to swing wildly around in time to see movement in the smoke.

Out of the choking smoke, an ovipositor buried itself in his eye. Lucas's eye burst as burning liquid pumped into his skull. They were upon him. Too many to track. Out of the gloom they came, the droning of their wings furious in its intensity. Crush one, and three more took its place, overwhelming him, filling him with burning noxious poison.

Lucas fell from the sky like the angels cast down. The wasps followed, the air vibrating around them, thick with their wrath. They covered him, biting, stinging, ripping him apart.

As sudden as the attack had started, it ended. They'd taken his eye, right arm to the elbow, both legs below the knee. His lifeblood ran out on the grass in stinking bursts pumped by his slowing black heart.

One landed on his chest, a giant wasp, larger than the others. The rest parted deferentially, making room. Clarity, the last he'd ever know, shocked him through the pain of his ruined body. She leaned close.

No more hunts, Lucas. Your fishing days are done. I want you to know who's killing you. The wasp's voice buzzed in his mind, at once alien and familiar.

Alicia?

Yes.

She jammed her stinger into his abdomen, pumping venom into his chest as she leaned in, and then her mandibles snapped his head free of his body.

The moon—bright, silver, beautiful. He knew he needed to act, but something was happening here. A message lay within the lunar vision, and he needed to hear it before he did anything else. The beast was coming, struggling to reach him, but it would never see these heights. This moon, with its shining radiance, spoke to him alone. Starlight sparkled in approval. For him alone. He was the reptile. He was Mark Branton. He was both. Unified under the light, he felt power filling him.

He'd led the monster to this place. This had always been the plan.

He'd never have defeated Lucas one-on-one, so he gave him to Alicia. He had wronged her—another her, in another life, under another moon—and it was for her to decide.

The light filled him, and he drew it in through his pores, into the spaces between his scales, the silver of his claws, his belly, the underside of his neck. The starlight lent strength, the moonlight wisdom. The Stonesong rang through his core.

He'd existed for millennia, millions upon millions of years, traveling down the generations and merging himself, Lord Reptile, with a human spirit counterpoint. Always bringing out the best in both. A defender. A protector. A survivor.

Wolf, bear, wasp, gargoyle, and other spirits ad infinitum circled his star.

Lord Reptile. The Night Dragon. The Black Scale. The names were many, but his essence was always the same. That was the Song. Brought out fully in the light of the moon, under the kiss of the stars.

Mark turned toward the broken gargoyle struggling to reach him.

No, little brother! Too soon!

He opened his mouth and released the light. A beam of pure life energy pulled from the light surrounding him erupted forth, scorching the earth and ripping across the offices of the Colony far below. The section of building exploded, throwing brick skyward, belching thick smoke and flame that obscured Lucas.

Defend the Colony!

The effect was immediate. The ladies of the Colony swarmed forth in their fury, believing Lucas responsible for the attack on their nest. As they did, Mark lost his hold on the reptile and fell a pale naked young man once again. Mark felt sharp pinching pains all over his body and a furious flapping of wings, thousands of wings, before losing consciousness.

Lexi felt them coming. Alicia wasn't far enough along in her evolution to detect the subtle changes in air pressure like she could. Striding from her office, Lexi willed the change upon herself. This Colony was ready for a new queen, new blood. Time to swarm. Start the cycle anew.

But first, the approaching interlopers had to be addressed.

Lexi thought they might bypass the Colony—until the explosion tore through her hive. Earlier, unsure why at the time, she'd pulled everyone away from the front of the Colony, even the drones. Not that any of that mattered now. They'd all survived the attack unscathed, and she sent the command: *Defend the Colony!*

The Colony's response was efficient and brutal.

They poured out, transformed, ready, and locked on the threat. They overwhelmed him with the sheer force of numbers, and Lexi left them to their fun, heading a different direction.

Lexi watched the boy's fall as the sparrows gathered in mass, arresting his terrible momentum, and bringing him gently to rest on the Colony's manicured lawn. She dispatched one of her guard to wade through the flock and collect the boy. Sparrows covered his body providing a warm feathery cover. Sparrows chirped their displeasure as she lifted the boy. Flapping around her, their dark eyes focused on the boy's limp form, she brought him to Lexi and laid him, unconscious, at her feet.

"Isn't this interesting?" Lexi said. The sparrows continued to hop on and off on Mark's chest.

Knowing she wasn't being addressed, the guard remained silent.

///

"There's someone here!" Trent Aleman called out.

The group of fire and rescue hustled over to assess the situation. A hand lay exposed among the rubble. The unbelieving crew sprang into action, removing debris as quickly as they were safely able. Trent, who'd been walking around the remains of their home in a state of mild shock, had noticed the hand when a pile shifted. He got out of the way so the responders could do their work.

"I thought you said there wasn't anyone in the house," a policeman said.

"There wasn't," Ciara answered for her father.

"Who is that guy, then?"

"Hell if I know. We were watching television when I thought I saw someone breaking into my car. Maybe he's the one."

"How'd he get inside?"

"How should I know? Nothing about this is normal."

The firemen removed the detritus above the old man. He was filthy, covered with dust. Blood mixed with dirt had hardened to a crust along one side of the man's face. He was completely naked, with a wild patch of iron-gray pubic hair. Ciara looked away, embarrassed.

"Why's he naked?" the policeman asked.

Becoming irritated with the accusatory questions, Ciara snapped, "Probably knew you'd be here."

A burst of laughter encouraged the policeman to save his line of questions for another time. Ciara shook her head at the cop's retreating back. Emergency medical services strapped the old man on a backboard, securing him in place. A large neck brace supported his head. As they loaded him into the back of a waiting ambulance, Ciara swore he tipped her a wink.

Mark opened his eyes to an unfamiliar room with stark white walls and an antiseptic smell in the air. Alicia sat next to him, reading a Stephen King novel.

"That the one with the psychic kids?" Mark asked.

"Yeah," Alicia said. "Decent read so far."

"Where am I? Hospital?" Mark tried to sit up.

"You're at the Colony in the infirmary. Lie back down."

Mark relaxed back onto the mattress. "How long have I been here?"

"Since you fell out of the sky two days ago." Alicia didn't look up from her book.

"Lucas?"

"Dealt with."

"Me?"

The door opened, and Lexi walked in. "What about you?" she asked.

"When can I go home?"

Lexi considered him for a moment. "Who gave you the stones?"

"I don't have them. Einar gave them to me but took them back."

Lexi seemed surprised. "He took them back?"

"Well, yeah. After the reptile chose me."

"A reptile chose you?"

Mark nodded. "Bit me right in the face."

"Mr. Branton, you are full of surprises. What was his name again?"

"He said his name was Einar. I don't know if that's his first or last name."

"What happened to him?"

"I dropped a house on him before I led the other one here."

Lexi bit her lower lip. "You got your vengeance and gave Alicia her justice. Granted, you did so by involving us in your schemes."

"There weren't any schemes other than I knew I couldn't beat Lucas alone."

"How do you know? You're Lord Reptile."

"He kicked my ass every time we met. I needed numbers. You wouldn't have helped without a direct threat to the hive. I'm not sorry I brought him."

"Are you sorry you drove him mad with Alicia's memories? Are you sorry for using the serpent stare on me?"

Mark opened his mouth to defend himself, but nothing came out. She was right. He'd used Alicia, Lexi, and the Colony. Mark believed it had all been for a greater good, but hadn't most evils been committed in the name of the greater good? He'd jeopardized he didn't know how many thousands of lives by bringing Lucas here.

Lexi interrupted his chain of thought: "It's been handled. The Colony is safe. A bigger concern is the stones."

The door opened, and a large Native American man led an equally large black man wearing wire-rimmed spectacles and two white women into the room. It was getting crowded in the small confines around his infirmary bed.

"Who are you guys?" Mark asked.

"I'm Axel," the Native American said. "This is Saul." He indicated the black man. "And Naomi and Charlotte." The women each inclined a head in turn. "We're from the council, and we are here to recover the stolen stones."

About the Author

Jeremy Eads was first published at six years old.

Since then he's gone on to be a traveling musician, soldier, spy, and software engineer.

You can find him on Facebook at OldSchoolScary or lurking over at Wicked House Publishing or Unveiling Nightmares.

When not writing, Jeremy is promoting novels, missing his kids, working on stories, more marketing, or writing.

He lives in southwest Virginia.

Acknowledgements

Many people are responsible for Reptile moving from my head to the page and into your hands. Crystal Baynam and the good people with Unveiling Nightmares who believed in a guy who lives in a cowfield enough to give him a chance. I hope I don't disappoint!

Also, enough credit can't be given to Mom who stayed with me when everything fell apart.

My wonderful children who kept me going.

Chelsea Cambeis for her solid guidance and tough love. Reptile wouldn't be what it is without her efforts.

Carmilla Mayes for her amazing cover design.

And Bianca Norton for being amazing.

The Lodge

A demon runs a bed and breakfast in southwest Virginia where sin never needs a reservation. A guilt-ridden retiree, two little boys, and a pair of meth-making cousins will challenge America's most wanted black widow, a haunted southern town, and the Devil himself. The quest for salvation will lead to the darkest parts of themselves as well as the beating black heart of Summit Valley, Virginia. The Maple Lodge, a B&B where the turndown service is to die for.

Made in the USA
Columbia, SC
12 April 2025